7 th December 1998

To Liz
from pauline,

Lynne Forrest

A PITY ABOUT MEN

Lynne Forrest

MINERVA PRESS
LONDON
ATLANTA MONTREUX SYDNEY

A PITY ABOUT MEN
Copyright © Lynne Forrest 1998

ISBN 0 75410 092 8

First Published 1998 by
MINERVA PRESS
195 Knightsbridge
London SW7 1RE

Printed in Great Britain for Minerva Press

A PITY ABOUT MEN

Chapter One

Amie glanced casually round her as she sipped a cool drink through a straw. There was lots of ice in the drink; also something stronger.

The view was pleasant. Not least was the prospect of her own shapely figure clad in a brief golden swimsuit. Her slim tanned legs were arranged sedately and becomingly as she lounged on a poolside chair. A blue and white striped scarf tied back her deceptively casual hairstyle, which had really taken ages to style.

This was the last afternoon of a weekend as a guest of the friend of a minor cog in the workings of a moderately important studio. The cog was actually only an assistant to the producer – but one step at a time!

Amie looked with curiosity at the other guests: no one very interesting. They were all on the make like her. Her present job was with a fashion magazine. After all she had to support her daughter, the product of a brief marriage that was best forgotten.

Then a new person came into sight. Her interest was immediately aroused. Just look at that tanned and muscular man! He was only of medium height but his chest was broad and his arms looked strong. He wore a brief swimsuit in a deep shade of blue.

The new arrival dived neatly into the rippling water, emerged shaking his head and performed a businesslike crawl to the far end of the pool. Amie took another sip from her drink as she watched him.

Looking round for her friend, Amie rose gracefully from her chair. There was her friend, Betty, walking along the poolside towards her.

'Having a lovely time, darling?' trilled Betty. This lady was one of those lucky creatures with perfect features, dimpled cheeks and honey coloured, meticulously tidy curly hair. The canary-yellow swimsuit she was wearing supported her slightly generous figure well.

'Hi, Betty,' murmured Amie. 'Could we have a walk-about? I'm becoming rather bored sitting around here.'

'Of course, babe,' responded Betty.

The two girls linked arms and set off in the direction of the house. They both wore strappy high heeled shoes to show off their legs to their best advantage.

The party was being held at a Spanish-style house in Hollywood. The pool in the grounds was surrounded by luxurious trees and vegetation. The two girls entered the welcome shade of the patio. Drinks were being served by two Mexican boys wearing smart white jackets and black trousers. Groups of guests stood chatting at the bar or lounged in easy chairs.

Betty sauntered to the bar and ordered drinks. Amie followed her and helped herself to snacks from the nearby buffet.

'Who was that man I saw swimming, the one with the tan and the blue swimsuit?' asked Amie when Betty brought the drinks over.

'Oh, him!' laughed Betty. 'Keep your eyes off him. He's spoken for.'

'Married?' queried Amie.

'No, but engaged to the producer's sister.'

Just then the man in question strolled into the shade of the patio, dressed in a bright casual shirt and dark shorts.

He walked across the patio directly towards Betty and kissed her on the cheek.

'Hello, sweetie,' he greeted her. 'How is everything? You look wonderful!'

Betty simpered. 'Just great,' she replied. 'John, I would like you to meet my friend, Amie. Isn't she just gorgeous? Amie, this is John Peters.'

'Great to meet you, Amie,' said John sincerely, squeezing her hand and holding her gaze with his bright blue eyes.

'Fine, how are you?' Amie replied, feeling overwhelmed.

'Let me introduce my business partner, Robert James,' said John.

Amie had not noticed that another man had entered the room with John Peters, as she was too occupied looking into those blue eyes. Glancing over John's shoulder, she saw a tall, thin man waiting quietly to be introduced. He wore a short-sleeved ecru cotton shirt and tan slacks.

'Pleased to meet you,' he said smiling, and shook hands with both the girls.

Amie looked briefly at him and nodded. The man of the moment for her was John.

'Hey, let's sit down and relax,' remarked John.

The four walked outside to where tables and umbrellas were grouped and selected an unoccupied table with four empty chairs. They relaxed in the shade of the umbrella, watching the swimmers cleaving colourfully through the azure water of the pool.

John Peters asked after Betty's family.

'Oh, Mom and Pop are fine,' she replied. 'I'm hoping to go back and see them one of these days.' There was a pause. 'How about Joanne? Where is she today?'

This speech was accompanied by a meaningful sideways glance at Amie, who was leaning slightly towards John, lost in the pools of his eyes.

'Oh, she's gone off with brother Bill, helping with the casting,' replied John, unfazed. 'What about this young lady?' he carried on, turning to Amie. 'Tell me all about yourself.'

Amie looked up at him from beneath the dark fans of lashes. His arm was draped casually across her shoulders, sending tingles through her body.

'Nothing much to tell,' she smiled. 'I work for *Clothes Horse*, the fashion magazine.'

'Tell me, are you somebody's child bride?' prompted John.

Amie laughed. 'You flatter me. I was married quite young and have a ten-year-old daughter. The marriage didn't work out and we divorced years ago. Poppy stays with my mother while I am at work,' she told him.

'You poor little thing!' exclaimed John.

'What do you do for a living?' Amie asked John.

'I'm sorry, Amie, I thought you knew. Robert here and I are accountants. Not very interesting I'm afraid but we get to meet the important and rich citizens of our great country,' John replied.

Amie was reminded of the presence of Robert James. He sat quietly by her side, listening intently to the conversation. Amie realised that Robert had not spoken since they had been introduced. He simply sat there with a quizzical expression on his face. Did he think himself above them?

Looking at Betty, Robert spoke. 'Do you ladies mind if I smoke my pipe,' he asked. 'A bad habit, I'm afraid, but I find the occasional pipe calms me.'

His voice was low with an English accent. Amie noticed his eyes were grey with little flecks of gold. The two girls replied that he should of course smoke his pipe. Betty later commented on his good manners.

The party eventually came to an end. The guests departed to their various pieds-a-terre. John kissed both the girls on the cheek and whispered in Amie's ear that she looked cute in her swimsuit.

Chapter Two

That evening Betty dropped Amie off at her house. Waving goodbye, she ran up the path and let herself in with her latchkey.

As Amie admired her tan in the hall mirror and ran her fingers through her light brown hair, she could see the need to wash and condition her tresses after the weekend spent outdoors.

Turning to look along the hall, she hung her jacket and purse on the coat stand. Then a small avalanche hurtled down the stairs and leapt upon her.

'Mommy, you're home!' cried a high-pitched voice.

Amie disentangled herself with difficulty.

'Wow, you're too big to climb on me now, honey,' she complained. Amie and her daughter, Poppy, sat on the stairs together.

'Have you been all right with Grandma?' asked Amie.

'Yes, but I missed you, Mommy,' moaned Poppy.

Amie cuddled her daughter and stroked her mop of auburn hair. Where on earth did she get that colour hair anyway? Certainly not from her. All those freckles, too!

'Never mind, I'm back,' said Amie. 'Let's go see Grandma.'

Amie and Poppy stood up and wandered hand in hand to the kitchen. A good-looking woman in her fifties was working away in there.

'I thought I'd find you in here,' said Amie, kissing her mother on the cheek.

'Just getting a little something for your supper,' answered the older woman. 'Did you have a nice time?'

'I'm glad I met Betty,' said Amie. 'We had a wonderful weekend and I've found a new group of friends.'

Walking back into the hallway she picked up her overnight bag and walked up the stairs. Poppy accompanied her mother to her bedroom and sprawled on the white satin bedspread.

Amie went into the bathroom and threw her used clothes into the laundry hamper. After putting her toilet articles in the bathroom cabinet, she undressed and stepped into the shower.

'How about a nice supper and a quiet evening,' she called out to Poppy. 'School tomorrow, you know!'

'Groan, groan!' called out Poppy.

Laughing, Amie finished her quick shower and dried herself off. Wrapping her bathrobe round herself and a towel round her hair, she padded back into her bedroom.

Poppy was sitting in front of the dressing table mirror, brushing her wavy red hair with her mother's hair brush. Amie stood beside her daughter, gazing through the window into the distance. Absently she twisted her daughter's hair round her fingers into ringlets. The little girl turned her head and gazed up at her mother.

'What are you thinking about, Mommy?' asked Poppy.

'Oh, nothing,' replied Amie. 'I just had a wonderful party and feel happy.'

Amie dressed herself casually in shirt and slacks and flicked a brush through her hair. Poppy held hands with her mother as they went downstairs for their meal. They ate in the kitchen. Evening was drawing on as the family sat round the table in companionable silence.

The room was decorated in cheerful yellow and white. Copper pans shone on the walls and decorative plates lined the shelves.

'What luck you are domesticated,' said Amie to her mother, 'I don't know what I would do without you.'

Rose Collins smiled serenely to herself. The yellow and white patterned curtains at the kitchen window behind her contrasted with her dark hair as she forked mashed potato methodically into her mouth.

'I always liked home keeping and raising children,' she replied. 'Now I have lost your father and your brother hardly ever writes there are just you and Poppy to look after. For the time being anyway,' she added meaningfully.

There was a silence, with both women lost in thought.

After the meal, Amie played cards with her daughter. Then it was bedtime for the young girl. Poppy moaned about going to bed but next day was a school day and she needed her rest. After the routine of bathing and hair brushing, the small girl, wearing her pink cotton nightdress, sprang with the exuberance of youth, into her bed.

'What energy!' exclaimed Amie, tucking her daughter in and kissing her goodnight.

Later that evening the two women sat companionably in their easy chairs in the living room. The television was on and they drank coffee as they glanced through the newspapers.

'Didn't you ever want to get married again?' Amie asked her mother.

Rose looked up enquiringly.

'What made you ask that?' she queried. 'Yes, there was someone I was friendly with a couple of years after your father went, but I had you children to look after. Somehow that didn't work out. After all, your father left me comfortably off so I could live without the support of a man.'

'Uh-uh,' muttered Amie, sipping her coffee. Fantasies featuring herself and John Peters were occupying her mind, so she was not really listening.

Just as she was thinking of retiring for the night, the phone rang. Rose answered the call and told Amie a man was asking for her.

Someone from the office perhaps, mused Amie to herself. Picking up the receiver she murmured, 'Hi.'

A voice vaguely familiar spoke to her. 'Howdy, Amie, this is John Peters.'

Amie's heart immediately leapt into her mouth. Breathing sharply, she demanded, 'How did you get my phone number?' feeling stupid as soon as she made the remark.

'That wasn't too difficult,' replied John. 'I enjoyed meeting you this weekend and hoped you were happy too.'

'Yes, of course,' said Amie, hoping her mother did not notice the steady flush impinging on her face.

'Although I didn't arrive until the last afternoon, I had a wonderful time,' said John.

'Yes, so did I, and was pleased to meet you,' said Amie, wondering what all this was leading up to.

'What are you doing tomorrow evening after work?' queried John. 'How about meeting for a quiet drink?'

Immediately, Amie pushed all thoughts of his fiancée and warnings from Betty to the back of her mind. 'That would be nice,' she said, trying to sound cool.

'I'll pick you up outside the office at six,' John responded crisply. 'I'll see you then.'

'Okay, fine,' said Amie. 'Goodbye.'

Putting the receiver down, she looked across at her mother. 'I'll be late tomorrow evening. Could you see to Poppy for me?'

'Of course,' replied Rose, merely raising an eyebrow.

Amie sprinted upstairs and threw open her wardrobe door. What should she wear? Best not something too dressy. A smart business suit should be all right for the office and a drink afterwards.

Quickly she selected a grey suit and white blouse. There was no need to wash her hair again. Putting her hair in rollers, Amie smoothed a mud pack on her forehead and cheeks. Locking the door, she lay on the bed and relaxed with her eyes closed for half an hour.

By this time she was ready for sleep, so she splashed her face clean, put on her pyjamas, and went to bed. The moon was visible in the corner of the window, and Amie gazed at the silver disc as she was lulled into sleep.

Chapter Three

Amie awoke to the shrill clamour of her alarm clock. Blearily, she reached out and fumbled on her bedside table for the alarm clock and pressed the off switch. This must be a workday. Suddenly she remembered the events of last night.

Leaping out of bed, she was galvanised into action. A hurried shower refreshed her. After quickly dressing, Amie flicked a comb through her wavy hair and applied lipstick to her sensuous lips. Proper make-up could be applied at work before going out in the evening with John.

Rose and Poppy were already dressed and sitting companionably at the kitchen table. Rose was sipping from her cup of coffee, while Poppy spooned cereal from a bowl.

'Good morning,' enthused Amie, then hoped she didn't sound too gushing for first thing in the morning.

Whilst pouring herself a cup of coffee, she glanced at her watch. There were just a few minutes for a slice of toast. Rose popped some bread in the toaster, reading her mind. Amie hoped her mother was not reading everything in her mind that morning.

As Amie sat tensely at the kitchen table, she nibbled on her toast and preserve. Why was she in such a state over a man? Also, why was she nervous of letting her mother know her feelings? If she was honest with herself, she had to admit feeling a bit guilty as the man had a fiancée.

Ever since her divorce, there had been no serious relationship in Amie's life. There had been men friends but she had not been with anyone since her break-up with her husband, Derek. Those acrimonious proceedings, not to mention his secret affairs, had left Amie hurt and mistrustful of men.

The advent of John Peters had brought Amie the first rush of feeling and emotions she had experienced for years. That was why she felt bewildered, almost like a teenager in the thrall of puppy love.

Amie realised she was gazing through the window into the distance again. Rose was watching her with a perplexed expression. Abandoning the toast and preserve, Amie gathered her things together for work. Poppy lifted her face to be kissed and Rose waved goodbye to her daughter.

As her car was being repaired, Amie ran down the road to the bus stop. Nearly time for the next bus. There were a few minutes to wait and then the vehicle chugged busily round the corner. The line of passengers filed aboard and were borne away to their day of work.

In the office the day progressed steadily towards lunchtime. Amie had plenty of work to occupy her. From her office window she could see the busy traffic scurrying to and fro, hooting noisily. Terrie, her secretary, who had an office next to hers, could be heard typing and answering the phone.

Terrie was a small pretty girl with black curls and sloe black eyes. Although she was a loyal worker, often her thoughts would stray to her boyfriend and she could sometimes be heard giggling on the phone to him. Amie overlooked her mild peccadilloes as Terrie was a good worker and her sunny disposition transformed the atmosphere in the office. Amie often wished she were as extrovert as her secretary.

Amie worked on in the office during her lunchtime. Mineral water and a sandwich served to stave off the pangs of hunger. The piles of advertising and photographs on her desk occupied her mind somewhat. Before long the quiet was invaded by the sound of the other staff clattering noisily into the suite of rooms after their meal.

The afternoon passed uneventfully. There was a meeting with the Finance Department concerning expenses. The afternoon coffee break and a snack gave her a welcome rest. Phone calls from advertisers and other clients took up the rest of the time.

At last leaving time arrived with Terrie hurrying out, breathless, to meet her boyfriend. The other staff left more calmly, calling 'Goodnight,' to Amie. There was time for a refreshing wash and make-up before John arrived.

Now that the moment had arrived, Amie felt nervous. Forcing herself to take slow deep breaths, she concentrated on getting ready. *You stupid fool*, she told herself, *this is just a quick drink with a new friend.*

What was the matter with her? All she felt right now was that she wanted to go home for a quiet evening. Perhaps he wouldn't turn up. What could they talk about?

Leaving the ladies' washroom, Amie walked back into her office. The intercom rang and the voice of the receptionist downstairs informed her that a gentleman was asking for her.

'Well here we go, my girl,' Amie told herself out loud, as she stepped into the lobby to ring for the elevator.

As she left the elevator, Amie spotted the smartly dressed man standing by the reception desk, his back turned to her and looking through the glass doors at the street. Warmth crept into her face. An effort had to be made by her to appear matter-of-fact. John Peters turned to face her as her high heels tapped in staccato rhythm on the parquet floor.

'Well hello,' he said cheerfully, shaking hands with her.

'Shall we go now, Amie? Hope I'm not too early!'

'No, not at all,' muttered Amie. I sound like a kid when in fact I'm the head of an office, she thought to herself.

John opened the glass door and the two emerged on to the evening street. Shadows were lengthening along the pavement and the last rays of the setting sun peered wanly over the rooftops. Taxicabs vied for business among the bustling crowd. In the plate glass windows of the department stores lining the sidewalk, reflections of the couple could be seen, keeping pace with them and mirroring their movements.

Her companion was wearing a charcoal-grey pinstripe suit, set off by a light blue shirt. He looked sharp and businesslike. Amie raised her hand to arrange her hair. This suit of hers with the short skirt showed her legs off to good advantage.

'Well, Amie, where shall we go for our drink? There's a little wine bar, Florio's, just round the corner,' said John.

'Florio's would be fine,' answered Amie.

John took her gently but firmly by the elbow and guided her through the homeward-going throng. Amie stole a sideways glance at him. He caught her look and grinned. His blue eyes crinkled at the corners and his white teeth contrasted with his deep tan.

'I hope you recognised me with business clothes on,' he said, laughing. 'You look very different.'

'You look smart in your suit,' said Amie.

John steered her down some steps and through a door into a busy bar. They found a table and John ordered some Chianti for them. The crowd left little room and they had to sit shoulder to shoulder. Amie felt the warmth of his breath as he leaned towards her and whispered in her ear.

'Darling, you look wonderful,' he murmured.

Amie felt her insides doing somersaults. The pounding in her chest must have been her heartbeat. This was ridiculous for a woman of her age; after all, they were not teenagers.

Nervously she forced a laugh. They looked each other in the eyes and she felt herself relaxing. John rubbed arms with her and shrugged apologetically. Glancing sideways at the crowd, he shook his head.

'This crowd should thin out pretty soon,' said John. 'Then I'll get us another drink to settle us down.'

True enough, the after-work drinkers soon began to trickle out. John and Amie settled themselves in a secluded corner. As bars go, this one was informal but comfortable and the lights were dim.

'When does your fiancée come back?' Amie blurted out abruptly.

Immediately, she could have bitten her tongue off. John flashed Amie a sharp look which stabbed her like a knife. To avoid his gaze, she fumbled in her purse for a cigarette. With shaking hands, she found her lighter, lit up and inhaled deeply.

'I didn't know you smoked!' remarked John, as if nothing untoward had happened. He glanced more softly at her and put his arm round her shoulders.

Chapter Four

'I don't smoke much. Only when—' she began.

'Only when you are nervous!' John finished her sentence. 'There is something wrong. You are not the same girl I met at the weekend. Why so shaky, honey? I am not about to eat you.'

'Am I so obvious?' queried Amie. 'This *is* different, as we just happened to meet at the party and this is planned.'

Amie stubbed out her cigarette in the ashtray. John squeezed her arm gently and she leant back against him, feeling more relaxed.

'That's better!'

John sighed, breathing in the perfume of Amie's soft hair. 'Now listen. For one thing, this engagement of mine with Joanne, that's not for real. Just business. For another thing, I saw you before you saw me. When I walked out to the poolside and saw your beautiful self decorating the scenery, I thought, that's for me! I dived in so you would see me and I wangled an introduction to you. When you walked by with those swaying hips of yours I could hardly keep my eyes off you. Not to mention your other lovely curves.'

Amie felt herself blushing scarlet. Deep inside she knew John was right. There had been this attraction from the start. Both of them had wanted to be together – and what could be wrong with that?

They forgot the time as they talked. Amie suddenly realised they had been together for two hours. John caught her looking at her watch. He pulled her closer to him and tightened his grip around her waist. Those penetrating blue eyes looked earnestly into hers.

'Are your eyes grey or green?' asked John, unexpectedly. 'All those little flecks in them are so attractive.'

'They're sort of in between,' Amie answered, looking down at her hands.

'Well, your lashes are thick and sexy. The more I see you the more I find to admire,' said John. 'By the way, you were looking at your watch. Are you hungry or bored?'

'Oh, never bored,' Amie hastened to explain. 'I told my little girl I wouldn't be too late.'

John stood up and helped Amie to move from the corner behind the table. 'Let's have a snack and I'll run you home,' he suggested.

'That's fine,' Amie answered.

John hailed a cab in the darkening streets. They went off to a restaurant John recommended, Max's. They held hands in the back of the cab. Amie was impressed he did not try anything else.

When they arrived at Max's, John leapt from the vehicle, held the door for Amie and paid the driver in one practised movement. The restaurant looked dim from the outside, with thick lace curtains draped across the wide windows, but candlelight could be seen glowing through them. John turned the brass handle and ushered his companion through the wood panelled door. Amie caught a glimpse of white cloth covered tables, each bearing a solitary red candle with flickering flame.

A short, dark-haired man, thick set and ugly, emerged from the darkness at the back of the room. He bustled forward, shaking his head. Amie noticed most of the tables were occupied. Perhaps there was no room.

'No room!' called out the man, echoing her thoughts. 'You must book ahead.' He peered closer. 'Oh, Mr Peters; I did not see you. Come, of course I have room!'

'Thanks, Max,' John replied easily, shaking hands with the proprietor.

'For you Mr Peters, no problem. And good evening, Madame,' replied the owner, glancing at Amie with a smile.

Max ushered the couple to a corner table. He bowed to Amie and pulled out her chair with a flourish. There was a lovely aroma of pasta and wine in the air.

'Aha, I see you appreciate the spaghetti, the minestrone!' exclaimed Max to Amie.

'Sorry we didn't book, Max,' interposed John. 'We just came on an impulse for a snack. Could we just have a nice bolognese and a bottle of house red? Is that all right with you, darling?' he directed at Amie.

'Yes, lovely,' replied Amie, blushing. He had called her 'darling' yet again!

The spaghetti bolognese was delivered to their table with a flourish. The ruby red wine complemented their simple meal. Amie felt an inner and an outer glow. John held her hand across the table.

Then their intimate whispered conversation was rudely interrupted.

'Good evening,' came a voice from behind Amie.

Looking over her shoulder, Amie saw the voice belonged to that annoying Englishman, John Peters' business partner. What was his name? Robert something?

'Hi, Bob,' John said, acknowledging the other man's presence without enthusiasm. 'What brings you here?'

'Just having a quiet supper,' came the laconic reply. 'Thought of going to a show but decided to go home instead. I saw you come in. I thought I should make myself known. Only polite, you know.'

'Draw up a chair and have a drink, Bob,' urged John.

Robert James hesitated and Amie felt his eyes on her. Why did he put her on the defensive? The waiter solved the problem by attentively placing another chair at the table. The tall slim man slowly seated himself.

'One glass then for me,' he agreed, 'I don't want to be the gooseberry.'

Amie glared at Robert. What a nerve the man had! What harm was there in a quiet dinner? After all John had said his engagement to Joanne was only business.

Robert James coolly returned her look. John laughed and made small talk about work. Amie wondered why she suddenly felt awkward. The atmosphere had grown cold.

'We didn't see you when we came in,' observed John.

'I know you didn't,' replied Robert. 'I was hiding away in the other corner with my thoughts.'

'Are you serious all the time?' asked Amie.

'I have been known to laugh,' replied Robert, a glimpse of a smile curving his lips. He ran his long slim fingers through his thick wavy hair. 'Well, boys and girls, I'm off,' he announced, draining his glass of red wine.

Robert rose to his feet, effected a solemn bow in Amie's direction, and left the restaurant.

'I wish that hadn't happened,' complained John. 'I didn't think he would be here.'

'Are you ashamed of being seen with me?' demanded Amie.

'No, of course not, honey,' John replied quickly.

The mood was broken. From a few minutes ago when the two were so close everything was spoiled. Amie sighed and gathered her purse from the table. John signalled to the waiter.

'Come on, let's go,' he called out; rather loudly, Amie thought.

As they left the restaurant, Amie shivered in the cool evening air. The wine had left her headachy. Also her feet were aching for some reason. Damn that Englishman, she thought to herself.

John put his arm around Amie's shoulders.

'I'll get my car and take you home. The office garage is not far from here,' he said.

'My head aches from that wine,' Amie told him. 'Perhaps I should get a cab.'

'Nonsense,' said John, forcefully. 'Come along and let me look after you.'

They walked in silence to where the car was parked and he drove her home. The mood was subdued on the way. When they parted John said he would call her. He kissed Amie firmly on the lips before he drove away, giving her no time to respond or reject him.

Chapter Five

Next morning rays of sunlight forced their way into Amie's unwilling eyelids, exploding with a vengeance into her throbbing head. The vibrating alarm shrilled through her brain like a sharpened knife. Carefully, she pushed back the tangled sheets to turn off the alarm. Somehow her face had become covered by a pillow.

What a change from the previous morning, when Amie had awakened eager to start the new day! Now the main objective was to get herself to the bathroom. Once there, she was sick in the toilet. Running the cold tap in the wash basin, she splashed cool water on her face.

That was enough washing for now. After drawing the curtains to shut out the light, Amie took herself back to bed. Some time later, Rose peered round the door and saw her daughter sleeping. With a rueful smile, she shut the door softly and went away.

Rose ran briskly down the stairs and into the kitchen. Poppy was seated at the kitchen table. Rose told her that Amie was not well and needed to sleep. The child munched her toast and muttered unintelligibly, her mouth full of crumbs.

Rose waited until Poppy had left the house for school. Then she phoned Amie's office and left a message that her daughter had a headache. For a while she pottered about tidying up. Later in the morning she popped out for some shopping.

When Rose arrived back with the groceries, she found Amie in the kitchen, drinking black coffee.

'Feeling better, dear?' she asked.

'Yeah, fine,' muttered her daughter, unconvincingly.

'Does your head hurt?' demanded Rose.

'I wasn't even out late,' complained Amie. 'We didn't even do much. I must have mixed my drinks. This isn't like me.'

'I think you have been run down for a while,' Rose replied. 'Why don't you go to the doctor?'

'I'll see,' her daughter retorted. 'I must go see if my car is ready. They must have done my repairs by now. Could you ring them for me, dear?'

Rose rang the garage and ascertained that her daughter's car was indeed ready to be picked up. Travel had been difficult for Amie without her own transport. At least that problem had been solved. The engine had failed a week earlier, causing inconvenience to the family.

Amie showered and took some medication for her hangover. Rose told her daughter she still looked washed out. True, her face was pale. This, together with her red-rimmed eyes, made her look like a wraith.

Later Amie went out, dressed in a casual sweater and jeans. There was no make-up on her face, apart from a little lipstick. A scrunchy kept her hair back from her face. The trainers on her feet made no noise on the pavement; just what she wanted – silence.

The garage was only two blocks away. The interior was dim and smelled of oil. Two men, wearing grease-smeared blue overalls, were working on a car. One of them looked up as Amie came in.

'Good morning, Mrs Blake,' said the man, wiping his hands on a greasy rag. 'Your car is ready for you.'

'Thank you, Joe,' said Amie. 'I'll write you a cheque.'

'That's fine,' said Joe. 'Say, you don't look too good. Had a rough night? Been drinking?'

'Something like that; I need some early nights,' replied Amie, ruefully.

There was some more banter between them before Amie climbed into her car and drove away. Driving relaxed her and she decided to go for a spin. Leaning back against the cushioned upholstery and not having the strain of standing any more, she gradually began to feel better. The breeze from the open window soothed her aching forehead.

After an hour's drive, Amie began to feel hungry; a good sign of recovery. Soon a café by the roadside came into view. Perhaps a snack would make her feel better. Amie pulled into the parking lot, found a place for her car, and entered the restaurant section.

Eggs and coffee were what she fancied. Amie gave her order to the waitress and soon was tucking into hot food. What she needed now was just to relax. All this business with her divorce, on top of having to look after Poppy and going out to work, was getting her down; not to mention her problems with John Peters. Luckily, her mother had come to the rescue.

As Amie stood up to leave, her eye caught a glimpse of a familiar figure. Looking quickly to the side, she saw Robert James, seated at a nearby table. Not that man again! Surely this could not be a coincidence. Amie stood immobile, undecided what to do. Robert James jumped up and strode over to her. Concern showed clearly on his face.

'Really, this is most unfortunate! I assure you I just happened to be here,' he explained.

They both sat down again at her table, in order to avoid looking conspicuous. There was a brief silence.

'You do seem to turn up wherever I am!' exclaimed Amie. 'Must be my fatal attraction.'

Robert laughed laconically and said, 'Not that you do not have a certain gamine charm in your clothes and hairstyle – but really, I was just out on business and called in here for some lunch. I hesitated to speak to you after the awkwardness of last night. My presence seemed to spoil the evening for you. In fact I felt rather guilty!'

This was the longest speech that Amie had heard Robert make. The tall man sat opposite her, a serious expression on his face. He looked quite smart in his navy blue suit and white shirt, Amie thought. He even had a thin moustache, which she had not noticed before.

'I didn't know you had a moustache,' Amie found herself saying.

'Well, that shows you haven't looked at me closely before,' replied the tall man, earnestly.

Amie felt herself blushing. 'I suppose I haven't,' she said.

'Nice to see some colour in your cheeks,' continued Robert. 'You looked like a ghost when you came in.'

'I had a rough night,' said Amie. 'Too much wine, I expect, so don't blame yourself for anything.' Robert was annoying her again. 'As to my look, I put these clothes on to pick my car up from the garage and decided to drive out to clear my head, which I have done, so now I shall bid you goodbye.'

Amie stood up and left for the parking lot, hearing Robert's voice coming from the restaurant behind her.

'What have I done to upset you now?'

Ignoring this plaintive query, Amie slid into her car seat and drove smoothly away, back towards home. What a cheek Robert had, continually engaging her in conversation. Anyone would think they were acquainted. The only lucky thing was that John Peters was not with him to see her in such a state.

When Amie arrived home, Rose's worried face was peering through the window.

'I wondered what had happened to you,' she said. 'You took so long coming back.'

'Oh, I'm sorry dear,' Amie said apologetically, kissing her mother on the cheek. 'I have been so selfish and should have called you. The day was so nice. I went for a drive and had some food at a roadside café.'

'Never mind, as long as you're feeling better,' said Rose. 'By the way, there are some messages for you. Terrie rang from the office and asked how you were. Also that man you were with yesterday, John Peters, phoned. I told him you were ill.'

Chapter Six

Amie spent the rest of the afternoon phoning the office to reassure Terrie she would be back tomorrow and pottering about sorting her clothes for work. While she was in her bedroom, the bed looked welcoming, so she lay down just for a minute. An hour later she was awoken from a nightmare, in which a monster with blazing eyes chased her down an avenue of tall trees, by the sound of her daughter chasing up the stairs to her room. Amie yawned, stretched, sat up and groaned.

'Are you better, Mommy?' demanded Poppy, whispering loudly in Amie's ear.

'Just as well I am, with all that noise going on!'

Amie laughed. Putting her arms round her daughter, she squeezed her tightly. Poppy nuzzled into her mother's neck and they both called out 'Aahh!' simultaneously. This was their playful routine. The two of them rolled on the bed, squealing.

Rose entered the room, laughing. 'I can hear you two children downstairs,' she chided.

They descended the stairs light-heartedly.

'Let's have a happy evening all together,' suggested Amie.

Poppy laid the table for supper, while Rose cooked the food. Amie picked some flowers for the table and arranged them in a vase. As it was Rose's turn to select the music that day, Frank Sinatra was crooning smoothly to them in the background. Poppy chose the sweet for after supper; strawberry ice-cream.

The little family sat down to relax after their meal. At eight o'clock the phone rang. Being the nearest, Amie picked up the receiver. Rose saw her daughter's face pinken slightly.

'Oh, hello John,' she said. 'Yes, all right. No, I can't. That will be fine. Not at this minute. I'll see you there.'

She put down the phone. Rose looked at her.

'Are you meeting that man again?' she asked incredulously, 'after all that last night!'

'That wasn't his fault,' explained Amie. 'Anyway I am well over twenty-one.'

The subject was firmly closed by Amie, who went upstairs. Poppy looked up from her comic.

'Is Mommy going out with a man, Grandma?' she asked.

'Yes, darling,' replied Rose, 'but not the right one!'

A meeting had been arranged with John Peters on Saturday. This time was going to be different. He had wanted to meet her again, so he must be sincere. They were going for a drive out in the country.

Amie woke up early on the day. The sun glinted brightly at her through the flower-patterned curtains at the window. Throwing open the window she breathed in deeply. A bird flew by, dipping a wing in greeting.

The rejuvenated young woman discarded her pyjamas and ran into the shower. A shower cap protected her hair, which she had put in pins. The warm water ran in caressing streams down her body. Rivulets of foam meandered down the hills and vales of her entrancing figure.

Amie quickly dried herself and applied body lotion and cologne spray. White satin underwear went next to her skin. The make-up and hair came next. Then Amie slipped a sky blue silk frock over her head. Tiny glass buttons glistened down the front of the sleeveless bodice. A wide belt hugged her narrow waist.

Amie looked at herself in the full-length mirror. 'You're not bad for an old divorcée mother,' she told herself.

Indeed this was true as the sun's rays crept through the window and played with the golden highlights in her wavy light brown hair. The paleness of her skin from the previous day had gone and the light tan of her face and shoulders set off the heavenly blue of her frock. A gold bracelet was her only jewellery. The swell of her bosom, her tiny waist and womanly hips made Amie a vision of loveliness. The flowing line of her skirt swished upwards as she spun round to show off her legs. Those legs were set off by gold high-heeled sandals.

John Peters was waiting for Amie round the corner. He was parked in his convertible, listening to his car radio. He sipped from a hip flask. As Amie came into sight, he put away the hip flask and waved a hand at her.

John Peters looked the young woman up and down appreciatively as he leaned over and unlocked the car door for her. Amie slipped into the seat next to him. He took her chin in his hand and pulled her face towards his. Their lips met for the second time, his mouth moving gently and rhythmically against hers.

Amie immediately went into overdrive. A sharp shaft of desire swept through her from pelvis to heart. Surely John could tell how she felt. With such a rapid heartbeat, Amie thought she could not survive for long.

John moved away from Amie. He looked deeply into her wide eyes; the irises were almost swamped by the expanded pupils. Kissing her swollen lips again gently, he stroked her cheek. The rapid rise and fall of her chest showed how fast she was breathing.

'Hey,' John whispered hoarsely in her ear. 'You do feel the same as I do! We must belong together.' He paused.

'Let's get away from here,' he said harshly, squeezing Amie's hand.

Putting the car into gear, John pulled away. He rapidly drove out of the suburbs into the countryside. Amie realised she had not yet spoken to John this morning but had been swept into feelings of immediate passion. The young woman turned to look at the stocky man beside her.

He was wearing a dark blue casual shirt and light tan slacks. His dark hair was brushed back. With a quick turn of his head, John flashed Amie a bright smile. Those blue eyes crinkled at the corners.

'We have to talk about the other night,' said Amie at last. 'Everything seemed to go wrong.'

'Sorry, honey,' said John dismissively. 'No one's perfect – and that fool Robert put me off my stroke, turning up like that.'

Now Amie had not meant that part of the evening. What worried her was the way John had reacted at the mention of his fiancée. There was a bitter taste in Amie's mouth and she suddenly felt let down. For some reason she decided not to mention her meeting with Robert James yesterday.

John was driving in the opposite direction to the one Amie had taken yesterday. Gradually the road was going uphill and a few trees dotted the roadside. The air became slightly cooler and Amie drew her light wrap round her shoulders. The few trees became many as the vista unfolded of hillsides below them carpeted with coppices.

'Let's put the top up,' John suggested, pulling over to the side of the road. He pressed a switch on the dash board and the top slid smoothly into position. The result of this was a warmer and more comfortable ride for Amie. Later they decided to park for a while where a spectacular view was spread out below them.

'I just want to stretch my legs,' he explained, getting out of the car.

'Good idea,' replied Amie, opening the car door on her side.

John walked round and took Amie's hand to help her alight from the car. They strolled through the trees to look down at the rolling view. Buildings and traffic were far away below, just like toys. Nature was all around the couple, with plants and hidden wildlife carrying on their secret activities.

'So, how are you feeling now?' queried John, seating himself on a massive tree root.

Chapter Seven

Amie sat down beside John, scuffling her feet through some fallen leaves. 'I feel wonderful now,' she replied.

'You look really marvellous,' John told her. 'I promise not to jump on you, but would you tell me something?'

'What is that, John?' Amie demanded defensively.

'How long ago were you divorced, darling? Tell me, have you been with anyone since then?' John squeezed Amie's hand and kissed her forehead. 'The way you responded to me was wonderful. You seemed as if you were hungry for love.'

Amie rested her head on her knees. 'I have been divorced for four years and have not been with anyone since then. For one thing I have my daughter to think about. For another I have not had any strong feelings for anyone.'

'Tell me,' John demanded, leaning towards her, his mouth close to her ear. 'Not until you met me. That's when you had feelings for me.'

'Yes, as soon as I saw you,' Amie replied. 'So now you know. Where are we going, by the way? I am getting hungry and thirsty.'

John stood up and helped Amie to her feet. 'Oh, didn't I tell you?' he said smiling. 'I have a place uphill a way.'

Amie raised her eyebrows. 'Oh, really!' she commented.

John drove the car progressively higher and in an hour they came upon a track leading off the road. This track led to a log cabin, nestling among the trees. A water barrel stood by the door. A pile of logs was at the other side.

'Home, sweet home,' announced John, taking a key from the glove compartment and opening the car door for Amie. 'Shall we go inside?'

Amie's breath was by now almost completely taken away. Allowing herself to be led to the door of the cabin, she stood there quietly, while he opened the door with the key. John entered first and stood aside for Amie to come in. He closed the door and lit a lantern.

'Quite a place you have here,' she remarked, trying to sound nonchalant.

'Not bad!' answered the man. 'Sit yourself down while I get something to eat and drink.'

The girl sat on a window seat while her companion busied himself lighting the fire and putting the kettle on. Before long a cup of steaming coffee was on the table before her. Cans of stew were emptied into a saucepan. The contents were soon simmering over the crackling fire.

Later, after the evening meal, they washed the few dishes together. The cabin was basically one room with a kitchen in one corner and dining space in another. The furnishings were sparse but adequate. A small bedroom led off at the rear. Toilet facilities were in a side cubicle. In front of the fire lay a thick rug.

'Are you enjoying your day?' John asked Amie. 'You see, I have not jumped on you! I only want you to be happy.'

'This is a lovely spot,' she replied. 'The day is still young. What shall we do? Can we go outside?'

'You won't do much walking in those shoes,' commented John. 'We can take a leisurely stroll if you wish.'

They walked out into the afternoon warmth. The sun was lower now and shone directly onto their position. This was indeed a lovely spot and far from the crowds and urban buildings. Amie felt relaxed and happy.

John looked at the slender woman by his side. 'You look happier than yesterday,' he said.

'I just want to stand here and breathe in the pure air,' she replied.

After a short while outside they returned to the cabin. John put on some radio music. He poured drinks and handed one to Amie. Comfortable chairs by the fire completed the cosy tapestry.

John finished his drink and came to sit on the rug by Amie's feet. As she sat there sipping her whisky and dry ginger, her companion slowly undid her gold sandal straps and removed them. He placed her feet one at a time on his knees and massaged them sensually. Wriggling her toes she sighed with delight.

'Are you enjoying this, honey?' asked John, softly.

'I really love a foot massage,' murmured Amie.

'I think there is room for two in that chair,' suggested John, quietly.

'Yes, maybe,' replied Amie, sleepy now.

John removed his shoes and squeezed into the big chair with her. He had to put his arm around her to fit into the chair. Amie could feel the warmth of his strong body against hers. His breath was hot against her neck.

Strangely, she felt unable to move. What paralysis was this? What was wrong with her coordination? Even time seemed suspended.

John broke the spell. 'Don't go all tense on me, Amie. All you have to do is turn your face round to mine.'

Amie turned her face to meet his. Their lips met as if to quench a terrible thirst. They must surely kiss forever to satisfy themselves. The stubble on John's chin rubbed against Amie's tender face, emphasising his masculinity.

At last they moved apart. Blue eyes gazed into green eyes.

'You're really something, darling,' gasped John.

'I've never felt like this before,' whispered Amie.

John caressed Amie's neck with his free hand and then slid his palm down past her shoulder. He touched her tender breasts gently and kissed her waiting mouth again.

John manoeuvred himself from the armchair and lifted Amie to her feet. He led her, unprotesting, towards the bedroom.

'Don't let's crush your beautiful outfit,' whispered the man even more softly.

John undid the glass buttons on Amie's bodice and slipped the blue silk frock to the floor. With eager hands he undid the white lace brassiere, which also fell to the carpet. He beamed with pleasurable anticipation as he removed his own shirt. Amie smiled as she ran her hands over the muscular chest she had wanted to touch at the party so long ago.

John bent to kiss her beautiful breasts. Amie ran her fingers through his hair and massaged his neck. He removed her briefs. Then they were both naked and his hands were pressing her against him, moving rapidly down her back to encompass her waist and hips.

Within seconds they were lying close together on the bed, muttering unintelligibly, kissing, with hands and lips everywhere. John could not wait any longer and he groaned with longing. Amie clasped her lover's strong back to her with urgently gripping hands. The rhythm of their love-making overtook him; he must possess her. This he did, with thought only for the heat of the moment.

Afterwards they lay together with pounding hearts. They breathed heavily and sighed with pleasure and relief. John laughed and kissed the tip of Amie's nose. This was an afternoon of passion to remember.

John leaned on one elbow to look at the window. 'I hate to spoil things but we must hit the trail before dark,' he remarked.

Amie picked up her clothes from the carpet and began to put them on. 'I think we have waited too long. Driving down in the dark might be dangerous,' she warned.

John had already dressed himself. He went out into the main room and then outside the cabin. Amie followed and stood beside her lover, linking arms with him. The cornflower blue of the sky above them had deepened to indigo, with stars beginning to glimmer in the firmament.

Chapter Eight

'Darn, you're right,' said John. 'We must have been too occupied to notice.' He swept Amie into his arms and began kissing her again. 'Do you mind staying the night with me? We can go down on Sunday morning,' he whispered huskily into her ear.

John led Amie back into the cabin and shut the door. He put another log on the fire and replenished their drinks.

'Looks like this is where I came in,' said John.

He drew Amie towards him, running his hands down her body. A new warmth grew in the pit of her stomach, ready to be fanned into a furnace.

'Let's relax in front of the fire,' whispered John, drawing Amie down on to the rug.

He brought cushions from the chairs to rest their heads upon. Amie lay with John's weight pressing down on her. He cradled her head in his hands and kissed her thoroughly. There was no possibility of not kissing him back – not the way she felt – and her passion led her to respond to him again fully and totally.

Later they sat naked before the fire and finished their drinks. The moon appeared in the window, etched against the dark sky. No one was about for miles to disturb the two of them. There was a feeling of freedom and abandonment in the cabin.

'This has been quite a day!' exclaimed Amie.

'Certainly has,' agreed John. 'I can't get enough of you. Shall we go back to bed? We can get better acquainted – or even get some sleep.'

'Well, I could do with some sleep,' Amie replied. 'Look at the time.'

John looked at his watch. 'We've had too much drink and too little sleep,' he agreed.

Amie went into the bedroom and crept into the bed. John followed her after damping down the fire. They snuggled down together, their limbs entwined. Soon both were sleeping soundly.

The intrusive glare of a bright morning teasing Amie's eyelids awakened her. John was already dressed and packing the car ready to leave. He came briskly into the bedroom. Perching on the edge of the bed, he took her hand.

'Come along, sleepyhead,' he boomed. 'We must get moving soon!'

Amie had yet another hangover. There were some head-ache tablets in her purse, which she took with the coffee John had made. Why didn't he ever get hung-over? Where were her sunglasses?

Before long, the cabin had been locked up and John began the drive back down the slopes. The winding road was bumpy. Amie's head was jolted every time the car went over a rough patch in the road. Funny she hadn't noticed that on the way up.

'I have to get back pretty quick, honey,' said John. 'There's someone coming in for a meeting. I'll drop you off at your home. Give you a call in the week, for sure.'

'Sure thing,' replied Amie. 'When my headache's better!'

John chuckled in an unsympathetic manner. After an uneventful drive down, Amie found herself being dropped off round the corner from her house. The thought of bed and rest beckoned. Lucky this was Sunday!

John gave Amie a quick kiss on the cheek and drove away before she had turned the corner. Quickly opening the front door with her key, she made her way upstairs and tumbled into bed without her mother hearing. Later she found out that Rose and Poppy were out visiting friends. Meanwhile Sunday afternoon was useful for catching up with her rest; she was asleep when Rose and Poppy returned to peep in at her later that afternoon.

When Amie awoke, darkness had come again. What had happened to the day? Some time seemed to be missing. Definitely she must stop drinking.

When would John phone her again, she wondered. *I've lost a day for him*, she thought hazily. Stretching her legs under the cool bedclothes, Amie yawned luxuriously. Better get up and see what the time was.

Outside the window, the moon floated majestically in the darkness. Gosh, an eternity seemed to have passed since she and John had looked at the moon through the window together! Yet conversely that event seemed only a few minutes ago. Stretching out her hand to her bedside table, Amie switched on the lamp.

The time was ten o'clock! Nearly time to go back to sleep again. Amie undressed, threw yesterday's clothes in the laundry basket and put on her night attire. Wearing a dressing gown, she crept down the stairs.

Her mother was pottering about in the kitchen. 'Aha!' she said.

'I'm so sorry,' said Amie. 'I have put you to so much trouble lately.'

'Never mind, dear,' said Rose. 'You can spend some more time with Poppy to make up. I put her to bed hours ago. I expect you got held up and couldn't get back last night.'

Amie put her arms round her mother and squeezed her. Rose listened to the edited story of yesterday. A frown creased her brow. The older woman looked into her daughter's face.

'Sit down and listen to me! I know this is none of my business but you have known this man five minutes and every time you see him you have some sort of trouble. He is no good for you. We were worried when you didn't contact us last night.'

'I'm really sorry, dear,' said Amie. 'I haven't been out for so long that I love to have a fuss made of me. We couldn't call last night. I promise to be more considerate to you and Poppy in future.'

Amie had a hot drink and some cookies before kissing Rose on the cheek and returning to bed.

Next day Amie got up feeling quite well and determined to be nice to her family. Poppy left for school with her gym clothes while her mother drove to the office. While parking her car in the private parking lot, she saw Terrie being dropped off by a handsome young man.

'Hi, Amie,' called the younger girl, walking towards her boss with her usual swaying gait. 'Guess what!'

Amie smiled indulgently at her secretary as they went up together in the elevator. Terrie was wearing a tight sweater and skirt with stiletto heels completing the outfit. There was a rosy glow on her cheeks. Unusually, her normally tidy brunette curls were tousled.

'My boyfriend proposed,' confided Terrie, her full bosom swelling even more with pride. 'We are now engaged.'

'Why, that's wonderful, Terrie,' said Amie. 'Let me give you a hug and wish you all happiness!'

'Gee, thanks!' said Terrie.

The elevator door opened to allow the two girls out. Terrie wiggled away proudly, her undulating hips swinging seductively. Amie sighed, feeling rather ancient and entered her own office. Another Monday was here and lots of work was on her desk!

Amie pressed the buzzer on her desk. Terrie hurried in with a cup of coffee for her boss. Already the girl's hair had been tidied. Lucky girl, her life was settled!

'Sit, do tell all,' invited Amie. 'When is the happy day?'

'We haven't decided that yet,' replied Terrie, perching herself on the edge of her chair. The younger girl crossed her plump legs. 'You'll sure get an invite though. You have been so good to me.'

'Was that him this morning?' asked Amie. 'He is very good-looking.'

'Mr Perfect, that's who I got,' giggled Terrie. 'Say, why don't you get married again? You're a doll! We could have a double wedding.'

Chapter Nine

John did not call that day, nor the next. Amie wondered whether she should phone him. Surely he must be thinking of her after that wonderful weekend. The days dragged endlessly.

At last Amie phoned Betty, her dizzy friend from the VIP weekend; which come to think was only two weeks ago. What a lot had happened since then! Betty was out of the office, but called back later. The familiar bubbly little voice exploded brightly from the phone and cheered Amie up immediately.

'Hi, Betty,' said Amie. 'Shall we meet for lunch on me? I want to thank you for taking me to that lovely house party.'

'Sure, babe,' replied Betty. 'Let's do that today while I'm free. I'm booked up all the rest of the week.'

A stream of giggles trickled from the phone. The two women arranged to meet at Toby's, a convenient restaurant near to the office. Amie hurried there, her thoughts in a whirl. Betty appeared ten minutes late, miniskirted and perfumed.

'Sweetie,' cooed Betty, kissing Amie on the cheek. 'What shall we eat? I'm famished.'

Amie was already seated at their usual table and was about to order. Betty selected her food and cheerfully chattered away as she munched her fries. Amie did not eat much, feeling too anxious to have an appetite. Betty eventually noticed this and questioned her friend.

'What's wrong?' she asked.

'Too many late nights!' replied Amie, ruefully.

'Say you haven't been out with that John Peters, have you?' queried Betty, shrewdly.

'Only for a drink,' admitted Amie. 'By the way, have you seen anything of him lately?'

'He hasn't been in our office, but say, that tall skinny sidekick of his was in the other day checking our accounts,' replied Betty. 'Now I think of that, he was asking about you.'

Amie felt a familiar surge of irritation at the mention of that other man: Robert James, of course. What on earth did he want? He was probably laughing at her from a distance.

'What did he want?' she asked.

The other girl replied, 'Oh, he just said', imitating the man's English accent, 'What a lovely afternoon he had at the party and what an attractive young woman my friend was.' Reverting back to her own accent, the girl said, 'Say, I think he's fallen for you!'

Amie tutted. 'He seems a peculiar man. I don't care what he thinks but I wish he would mind his own business. So you haven't seen John,' she said, reverting to what to her, at that moment, was of the utmost importance.

'He's probably gone away with his girlfriend,' commented Betty. 'I told you to keep your eyes off him.'

'I don't think that engagement is serious,' protested Amie.

Wild jealousy raged through her at the thought of John being with another woman. The thought had not occurred to her. The man's casual dismissal of his engagement as nothing had seemed sincere. Anyway there was no proof he had gone away with her.

'Well, I have to get back to work, sweetie,' remarked Betty, bobbing up and smoothing her stockings into place.

Amie paid the bill and followed her friend out into the street.

'Don't forget what I said: forget that man, he's trouble!' were Betty's parting words as she sauntered away along the sidewalk.

Amie returned listlessly to the office. Even Terrie's good humour failed to lighten her boss's dark mood. Why hadn't John rung her? Perhaps because her remarks when they parted had been sharp.

Like those who have been infatuated through all time, Amie went over her every word and action with John, wondering what had gone wrong. Now another weekend was upon her. What could she do with herself? There was nothing exciting to do.

Betty phoned Amie at home on Saturday morning. Apparently Robert James had been in her office on the Friday afternoon and Betty had remarked that she had just lunched with Amie. On hearing this, the tall man had asked whether he could have permission from Amie to meet her some time. He wanted to discuss something.

'Can't that guy leave me alone?' retorted Amie. 'He's always looking over my shoulder.'

Robert James did phone Amie soon after that. He asked to meet her and said he had something to tell her. Eventually she agreed to meet him. On Sunday morning they met at the café of their previous encounter.

Amie drove there, her hair tied back with a scarf, and wearing a casual top and jeans. The breeze eased her mood and before long she drew up outside the café. There was a battered old Ford outside. Of course that would be his!

Having entered the room, Amie paused while her eyes grew accustomed to the dimness after the sunlight outside. The solid wooden tables and chairs created a folksy atmosphere. The check tablecloths brightened the room. There, at his corner table, Robert James awaited her.

He rose to his feet and pulled out a chair for Amie. The proprietor bustled over to them. He took their order for coffee and doughnuts. There was a short silence.

Robert James coughed nervously and stroked his moustache. Surely he wasn't scared of her! Amie looked down at the tablecloth. Forcefully, she drew patterns on the canary-coloured material with her fork.

Amie looked up at Robert. 'Well!' she said. 'What do you want now?'

Robert hesitated. 'Look,' he said. 'I say, you do look attractive in that turquoise sweater.'

Amie was rather taken aback. 'Thank you,' she said.

Robert took a deep breath. 'I want to warn you about John Peters. Just hear me out. There are things I must tell you. This man is a great friend and colleague of mine and was a help to me in England two years ago when I had some trouble. Anyway, I can't help seeing what a decent and vulnerable young woman you are. You cannot trust this man and I know you are attracted to him. I can see you getting more deeply involved when you mean nothing to him.'

'I am putting this badly, but John goes from woman to woman like a bee from flower to flower. Whenever I see you together I cannot say anything but I know you are becoming more unhappy. Also... there is his fiancée, who is extremely clinging. Forgive me for putting you through all this but I don't want to see you get hurt.'

There was another silence. Robert fingered the lapel on his rough tweed jacket and sipped at his coffee. There was no noise at all in the café. Amie looked up at the tall man.

'I am sure you mean well,' she replied, controlling her feelings with an effort. 'However, I feel my affairs are my own business. I wonder why every time I turn round you are there watching me, passing judgement. Do you know, I feel like a specimen on a slide! Whenever something goes wrong you are there watching me.'

'I assure you', replied Robert indignantly, 'those occasions when I have been in the same restaurant as you have been mere coincidences and I shall endeavour not to let that happen again. My intentions were good. Excuse me!'

He stood up abruptly and left the café, his long legs carrying him quickly from the room. Amie heard the loud engine noise from his battered old Ford as he drove away. So he did have a temper, too! Also, she'd been left to pay the bill!

Chapter Ten

Next day Amie was almost relieved to get back to work. At least her mind would be on other things. Terrie was her usual bubbly self, completely absorbed with her forthcoming wedding.

John did actually call her that Monday. He said he had been out of town and had missed her like mad. Unfortunately he couldn't see her for a couple of days: there were lots of important meetings in his diary.

Then, almost immediately, another call came through for Amie. A woman's voice spoke to her; someone she didn't recognise.

'Mrs Blake?' queried the quietly confident voice.

'Yes, who is this?' replied Amie.

'My name is Miss Joanne Webber,' came back the reply.

'I'm sorry, you seem to have been put through to the wrong office. I don't know you,' said Amie, puzzled.

'We do seem to have something in common,' replied the coolly arrogant voice. 'My fiancé. You do know him. John Peters. Could we meet in order that I might point out a few things to you?'

Amie felt herself blushing scarlet. What could she do but play for time in order to pull herself together? Someone had obviously been telling tales. This engagement was more serious than she had thought, or this woman was as clinging as someone, Robert James, had said.

Breathing deeply, Amie said, 'I can't see what your affairs have to do with me. I am too tied up to speak to you at the present time, so would you excuse me?'

'To be blunt with you,' said Joanne Webber. 'I know you have been playing around with my fiancé. You are not the first one and things can be made very difficult for him – and for you.'

'Goodbye, Miss Webber,' said Amie. 'I have nothing to say to you at the moment.'

As she put down the receiver, Amie realised she was shaking with emotion. What was happening to her? Suppose someone had listened on the extension? This was not meant to happen to her!

With trembling fingers, Amie lit one of her rare cigarettes. Terrie breezed into the office, looking unconcerned and bearing welcome coffee. The girl frowned and shook her head disapprovingly at her boss at the sight of her smoking. There was a politically correct rule in the office against smoking so the cigarette had to be stubbed out; she didn't want one anyhow!

Amie waited until Terrie had left and picked up the receiver again. John's office number was in her desk diary. He must be told what had happened. His voice answered after four rings.

'John, we must meet. Something awful has happened,' gasped Amie.

'Of course, my darling,' came the reply.

Amie immediately felt herself relaxing and bathing in the reassuring sound of his voice.

'Meet me outside tonight after work,' said John and put the phone down.

That evening Amie hurried to the elevator and travelled down to the ground floor. Pushing open the glass doors, she could see John waiting for her. They walked together round the corner to a dark alcove. They put their arms round each other and kissed, slowly and passionately.

This was not supposed to happen. Amie could feel the rough bristles from John's chin on her face. Oh, what a relief it was just to kiss him and think of nothing else! He groaned, burying his nose in her hair and caressing her neck with his lips.

'Oh, darling,' she whispered.

'My lovely baby, I missed you so much,' he murmured. 'I couldn't see you last week. We'll make up for lost time, believe me.'

Amie stroked the back of his hair and gently massaged his neck. John held her tightly and moulded her body against his.

'John,' Amie endeavoured to regain her composure. 'That woman phoned me today soon after you did.'

'Woman?' John said, and moved away, his tones harsh. 'You don't mean Joanne!'

'I didn't know whether you knew,' said Amie. 'I don't like being threatened.'

'I thought you called me because you missed me so much you couldn't wait to see me,' said John. 'Now this!'

Amie felt miles away from John. Why did he always make her feel in the wrong? He needed to be told what had happened. Perhaps he could be persuaded to put his arms around her again.

Then her wish came true and she found herself crushed by his strong embrace. His hands pressed her tightly against him until she could hardly breath. Their mouths met and their lips moved gently together. They swayed slowly and rhythmically.

'I hate to be away from you,' whispered Amie against his face.

'I didn't mean to yell at you, honey,' said John, kissing her again. 'Look, we must get together again and think what to do. Next weekend, get away and meet me. I'll sort out a place to go.'

They held hands as they walked back to the lights of the street. Agreeing to speak during the week, they parted, each to go home separately. Amie felt weak and dishevelled. John had not said much about Joanne Webber, after all.

When Amie arrived home, she parked the car in the garage and let herself into the house.

'Hello, everyone,' she called out.

'Hello, Mommy,' came a child's reply from upstairs.

Poppy came sliding down the banisters and landed in a heap on the hall carpet. Amie laughed and patted her daughter on the cheek. The little girl straightened her green sweater and blue jeans as she stood up. They hugged each other and went into the kitchen.

'You're late,' said Rose, turning round from the cooker. 'I thought the dinner would spoil.'

'We have pot roast', whooped Poppy, 'my favourite!'

'I was held up at the office,' Amie said to her mother, almost smiling to herself at the corny phrase usually reserved for spouses.

They sat at the table. Amie produced a bottle of white wine from the fridge. This was sorely needed after the day she had today. Even Poppy had a little drop.

'This makes me sleepy!' exclaimed Poppy.

'You can go straight to bed after dinner,' said Amie.

Poppy was allowed to watch television for an hour and then went obediently to her bedroom. Amie tucked her daughter up in bed and kissed her smooth white forehead. Freckles were sprinkled on her upturned nose. Old Teddy watched balefully from the bedside chair.

Amie sighed and wandered into her own room. Would her relationship with John work out? Hurry and be here, weekend. Let me see him again, she murmured to herself. The shower beckoned enticingly. Throwing off her clothes, the young woman stood beneath the flow, letting the rivulets run down her face and body, trying to lose herself in meditation; tomorrow would come soon enough.

Chapter Eleven

Rose Collins was worried about her daughter. The usually sensible young woman was behaving erratically. Of course she was entitled to a social life but all this staying out late and moodiness showed an underlying dissatisfaction, not happiness.

Amie was a grown woman and Rose could do nothing more than stand aside and be there when she was needed. The older woman had not entirely altruistic reasons for wishing her daughter to be settled with some steady man. Each of us can be lonely for companionship within our own age group. Those who are older than fifty do not necessarily wish to stay at home, caring for relatives and having no life of their own.

Rose belonged to several clubs, which she attended whilst her daughter was at work and her granddaughter was at school. A woman came in to clean, leaving Rose free to go out after having done the shopping and laundry. Sometimes she would meet friends at various social clubs. A particular venue she enjoyed was in rooms above a department store in town.

There, respectable tea dances took place. Mixed groups sat at the tables to relax. Fraternisation led to friendships. The musicians played discreetly in the background, whilst the patrons danced or conversed as the mood took them.

Rose liked to keep her hair short but well styled. A few grey hairs contrasted with her brunette colouring. The slim girlish figure of her twenties had filled out, but not too much for her taller-than-average height. Deep blue eyes gazed shrewdly but serenely from her pale-complexioned oval face.

Together with her close friend and near neighbour, Wanda Merrington, Rose liked to dress up, do her make-up, put on her high heels and socialise at this ballroom. There the two women had made friends of both sexes. This was preferable to staying at home with the television. Eventually there was a group which gravitated together to share a table.

Rose's particular man friend at these dances was George Lestrange, a retired lawyer. The two friends enjoyed ballroom dancing together. Being almost six feet tall, silver-haired and a good conversationalist, he was an ideal companion for Rose Collins. He was a divorced man whose grown-up children had moved away.

Rose's friend, Wanda, was shorter and plumper than her; a jolly, friendly woman. All was style about her, from the brushed-up blonde hairdo piled in curls on the top of her head, to the fashionable glossy bronze court shoes on her neat little feet. That jolly manner concealed a sarcastic wit and a sharp business sense. This lady was also a widow.

Wanda's husband had been in business and had left her well provided for. Some of this money was invested in stock or property. Now she had her eye on a new marital prospect. This was her dancing partner at the tea-rooms.

Fred Martin was a portly, balding man, fond of his food and drink. Owing to his success on the Stock Market, he was well able to satisfy the wishes of any current wife. As he was divorced at the moment, Wanda was hoping to be the next Mrs Martin.

The four of them sat at their favourite table, the day after Amie had that momentous conversation with John Peters. Rose wore a simple, belted linen frock of pastel blue with long sleeves and Peter Pan collar. Wanda's ensemble consisted of a fitted purple moiré silk suit with peplum. A lace cravat peeped from the discreet neckline.

Fred Martin beamed across the table at Wanda. He wore a dark blue suit, complete with waistcoat and gold chain spread over his substantial middle.

'Shall we?' he requested, bowing gallantly to Wanda.

'Absolutely delighted,' responded Wanda, rising surprisingly lightly to her feet.

The two of them danced gaily away together, chattering merrily. George turned to Rose and spoke earnestly.

'Fred and Wanda certainly make a fine couple,' he said. He took her hand and gave a little squeeze. Rose smiled at him.

'Remember what we were talking about? Couldn't we make a permanent union?' pleaded George.

'You have asked me this several times,' replied Rose. 'You know there's nothing I'd like better but I can't leave Amie at the moment.'

George sighed. 'I wish your daughter would remarry so that we could be free to do what we want.'

Rose looked up at the handsome man in the dark grey suit. 'Dear, you're wonderful to be so patient.'

'Come on, you two!' called Fred from the dance floor, as Wanda waved over his shoulder. 'Have some fun like us!'

Rose looked at George quizzically. They stood up, still holding hands. Smoothly they went into each other's arms. As they glided easily into the dance, their faces brushed together gently.

When the dance came to a conclusion, Fred suggested a drink in a bar. Wanda enthusiastically agreed and everyone left, bidding friends adieu. The two women slipped on their outdoor jackets. George pulled Rose towards him and kissed her on the forehead.

'Come to my place afterwards,' he muttered. Rose nodded. The little group went to a nearby bar, the Diamond Star, for cocktails.

'I'll get these,' Fred called out as they entered the door.

Rose and George sat together in a corner seat, holding hands.

'Oh, you two lovebirds!' chortled Wanda. 'Give that a rest.'

Rose blushed and moved away. Fred brought the drinks over to the table, remarking that he could not stay long anyway as he had some business to attend to.

'You can give me a lift, honey,' Wanda told him, sipping daintily from her glass and winking at Rose.

George bought the next drink. With everyone promising to meet again next week, the party eventually broke up. Wanda left holding Fred's arm possessively. Rose waved goodbye to her friend.

'I have to get back soon to get the supper,' said Rose.

'You can come home with me first,' demanded George. 'The children can wait.'

George went to get his car. He helped Rose into the front seat and drove her to his service apartment, which he used while in town. Having parked his car they ascended in the elevator together. They kissed, breaking off as the doors opened on to his floor.

George took his key from his pocket and opened the door for Rose. Kicking her shoes off, she threw herself on to the luxurious brown velvet sofa. Matching lined curtains covered one side of the room, reaching from ceiling to floor. The fitted carpet was beige.

George removed his shoes and jacket before collapsing next to Rose on the sofa. He propped his feet up on the coffee table in front of him and put his arm round his companion.

'I guess Fred and Wanda know we come here after dancing,' remarked George.

'Well, we aren't kids', replied Rose. 'We don't know what they do themselves.'

'They haven't known each other as long as we have,' replied the man.

'You talk too much!' retorted the woman.

George covered Rose's mouth with his own and began to undo her collar.

Chapter Twelve

Amie heard from John eventually. He called on the Thursday and asked her to meet him on Saturday morning to go to the hill cabin again. They would take some provisions. Happiness would be theirs!

There was only one day to get ready. Amie decided to take casual clothes this time, as they would be more suitable for the rough terrain up there. The next evening she rooted through her wardrobe. A white sweater and pink cotton trousers worn with socks and tennis shoes would be acceptable.

A jacket for the evening chill was selected; a black one. Perhaps her new green silk sleeveless knee-length gown would be good for the evening too. The little weekend bag was packed quickly, ready for the morning. There only remained the selection of shoes for the night and her cosmetics and she was ready.

Rose's voice drifted up the stairs. 'Amie, phone. A man for you.'

Amie jumped nervously and ran her fingers through her hair. Oh no, something had gone wrong!

After almost tripping as she ran down stairs, Amie picked up the receiver. 'Hello, who is that?' she asked.

'Robert James,' came the voice. 'I hope you don't mind.'

Oh no, not now! Amie's spirits sank immediately.

'I thought you were – never mind,' she faltered.

'Look, this is just to say I did not mean to offend you the other day. The intention was to help you, not interfere,' he explained. 'Walking out like that was rude. I should have been more considerate in the circumstances and I wish to apologise.'

'You certainly do talk once you get started,' remarked Amie. 'When I first met you I thought you were reserved and stand-offish.'

Robert chuckled. 'I can be nice when you get to know me.' His voice was warm and friendly.

Yes, just like a puppy, thought Amie to herself. Aloud she said. 'Well, thanks for your apology, Robert. Buying you a coffee was the least I could do after all your trouble.'

Without waiting for a reply, she firmly replaced the inoffensive receiver. Immediately she felt a bit guilty. Maybe she had been too flippant. The poor guy was only trying to be helpful.

'Mom,' called Amie, hurrying to the kitchen. 'Look, I'm going away for the weekend. Would you mind looking after Poppy for me? I think she's staying with her school friend, Jane on Saturday night. You won't have too much to do.'

Rose sighed to herself. 'That's fine, dear. Just enjoy yourself and don't come back with a hangover,' she said.

Amie laughed, ran out of the room and skipped up the stairs. 'Look at me acting like a teenager! Act your age, girl,' she scolded herself, all the time not really caring.

Poppy looked out from the bathroom, her hair dripping wet in tendrils over her thin shoulders. 'Keep the noise down! You're disturbing me,' she ordered mock sternly.

Amie grabbed hold of her daughter and began to dry her hair with a snowy white fluffy towel. 'You are so beautiful,' she growled in a deep voice, enveloping the child in a bearhug, as Poppy stood there laughing in her white cotton petticoat.

Rose stood downstairs, listening. 'Mark my words, Amie, my girl, like I told you when you were a little girl: too much excitement and there will be tears before bed-time,' she said quietly to herself.

Saturday morning came and Amie woke early. The light filtered weakly through the lace-covered window. Outside, a little lone bird voice was twittering gallantly to summon the dawn. The breeze rustled through the leaves, nudging the branches and causing them to tap gently on the window pane.

Putting on her clothes was the work of a few minutes and she made a thermos flask of hot coffee for the journey, then let herself quietly out of the house. Once outside she found her lover waiting in his car round the corner. They kissed briefly as the young woman slipped into the front seat. Then the man drove smoothly away from her neighbourhood.

'I got away all right, and brought some coffee,' said Amie.

'Good, we'll stop on the way for some,' replied John.

They did not speak much on the drive. Amie rested her head on the seat back and put her hand on John's knee. Smiling to herself, she thought she would not have done that on their previous drive to the hill cabin. There was a certain reassurance in the feel of his solid and sturdy legs beneath her light touch.

John chuckled and squeezed Amie's hand. They took a break at the same spot at which they had stopped on their first visit together to the wilderness and sat on the same massive tree root to drink their coffee. Then they strolled among the trees to stretch their legs. The morning was not as far advanced as the last time they had rested at this place and they would have longer at the cabin.

'Come on,' urged John presently. 'One last lap and we'll get there for lunchtime and I'll have you all to myself.'

'Race you to the car,' replied Amie sprinting ahead.

After an uneventful drive, they arrived at the cabin and John opened the door. Amie walked in stretching her arms out luxuriously. What a long time since they had been there! At least that was her impression, although in fact the interval had been only a few weeks.

John followed her in, carrying a carton of food and wine. Amie began to unpack, while John lit the fire. The real celebrations would be that evening. A dinner and drinks in style would be the climax their break away together deserved.

John sat in the big armchair. Amie perched herself on his knee and ran her fingers through the dark hairs on his muscular arms. His tie was promptly loosened by her and his shirt buttons undone. Slipping her dainty hands inside his shirt, she stroked his sculpted torso.

John grasped Amie's waist and pulled her towards him. Their lips met in a long kiss. Without a word, they got up from the big chair. Hand in hand, they walked slowly into the bedroom.

Some time later they surfaced from the bedclothes. John stretched and yawned. Amie leaned on her elbows and rested her face on his chest. He caressed her fine, light brown hair.

'How about a stroll round the property?' suggested John. 'I could do with the rest. You surely are a loving girl!'

'Well, only with you,' said Amie sharply. 'Are you suggesting anything?'

'No, of course not,' soothed John.

'All right', agreed Amie, 'a walk sounds good.'

Their clothes were scattered randomly on the carpet. They put them on and ventured out into the afternoon sunshine.

'John, that partner of yours, Robert James...' began Amie.

'What about him, honey?' asked John.

'Have you known him long, and why has he come here to live?' she queried.

'He's a strange guy, quiet but dependable,' replied John. 'I met him in London through friends when I was there on business some years ago. He had been through a rough time. He lost his wife and kids in an accident and I think he blamed himself.'

'I didn't know that. How terrible!' Amie exclaimed.

The man narrowed his eyes and gazed out over the treetops beneath him. 'Seems Veronica was driving the car in bad weather conditions when a big truck crashed into them,' he continued. 'The truck driver had been taken ill at the wheel and did not survive either. Robert can't come to terms with what happened.'

Amie could only gasp and say, 'Oh, no, the poor man!' To think she had been rude to him when he had been through so much...

Chapter Thirteen

Although Amie tried to put John's revelations about Robert out of her mind, the vivid picture came back at intervals of the devastating scene from the past. By telling herself these things happened all the time, the fact that this tragedy affected someone she knew did not make the accident any more sad than if he had been a stranger, the young woman managed to dismiss her depression. The weekend must not be spoilt. The companionship of the man she was with was everything.

John and Amie strolled higher up the slope. All their energy was needed to keep up an even pace. Squirrels ran swiftly from forest floor to branches with effortless speed at the humans' approach. Inquisitive grey faces peeped down from the safety of the canopy above at the two intruders.

Soon the cabin was out of sight among the trees below. Only a wisp of smoke, curling from the chimney into the clear air, betrayed the position of their little rendezvous. A grassy bank provided a welcome resting place after the arduous climb. They must have been walking for about an hour.

Amie, who was winded, lay down and placed her folded jacket beneath her head. 'I need a rest,' she gasped.

John too was breathless and he lowered himself to the ground. 'At least the way back is downhill,' he said, and laughed as he threw stones and twigs down the hillside.

John turned to look down at the face of the young woman lying beside him; her eyes closed. The exertion had brought a healthy glow to her cheeks, and her hair, slightly tangled by the breeze, was spread out, catching the last rays of the sun on the golden highlights. An ant ran briskly along the sleeve of her sweater, in a hurry to get somewhere. The front of her white sweater rose and fell rapidly, as she tried to get her breath.

'You are gasping for air,' said John. 'Did I go too fast for you?'

'No,' replied Amie, eyes still shut. 'I can keep up with you any day.'

John pounced on Amie and tickled her ribs. They both collapsed, laughing. His hands moved upwards to caress the swell of her bosom. He pulled up her top and removed her trousers.

'Let me have you now, out here in the wild!' John exclaimed, roughly massaging her shapely body.

'Take your clothes off, too,' Amie gasped.

The man threw them off and lay down on the young woman. He raised her lower back, with one hand supporting her. With the other hand he traced the contours of her breasts, pressing down hard. He kissed her face and mouth as they made love. She wanted the experience to last forever.

As John's weight relaxed on Amie's body, she realised stones and twigs were hurting her back. The man rolled away from her, breathing heavily. As they dressed, he patted her bottom, which she found irritating. The evening air was becoming cold.

'Down we go to get warm,' said John, taking Amie by the arm.

The scramble back down the hillside did not take too long, and soon they were back within sight of the cabin. A shower refreshed them; although there was not much space with two of them in the cubicle. They embraced tenderly but not passionately as the warm water caressed them. Hunger had begun to gnaw at them, so they dressed, and began to cook the dinner.

John admired Amie's green silk outfit. He wore a dark navy suit. As the delicious food was cooking, the couple toasted each other with chilled white wine. Then they walked outside to breathe in the sharp air.

Amie picked some wild flowers for the table. A glass served as a vase. They were becoming quite domesticated. Their future could be together!

'This has been a wonderful day,' sighed Amie, as she consumed her pie and potatoes hungrily. 'Are there any more broccoli and carrots?'

John squeezed her hand. His eyes crinkled at the corners as he smiled at her, saying, 'Leave room for your dessert.'

'We can eat the fruit later,' replied Amie. 'Being happy always makes me hungry.'

John laughed, 'Don't start putting on too much weight. I like you as you are.'

Amie realised he didn't say 'love'.

'I have had enough,' she said, pushing away her plate. 'Let's get washed up.'

'You know what, honey,' John remarked. 'You are changeable, and I must say I like the change in your loving – you're not as tense as you were!'

'Why analyse my feelings?' Amie almost snapped. 'You don't understand at all how I felt.'

John held his hand up defensively. 'I knew you were like a time bomb waiting to go off when the right man came along.'

There seemed to be no answer to this platitude. Why was John so insensitive, when she thought their instant attraction had brought her feelings to the surface? He seemed to think she was a frustrated female looking for a male. This was not the truth, but probably just what men *would* think.

Amie felt quite sober and thoughtful for the remainder of her stay in the cabin. That was in spite of the consumption of several bottles of wine. Things seemed different now; not wild and reckless any more. That evening she sat on the rug before the fire, sipping at her wine and gazing thoughtfully into the changing red and grey kaleidoscope of the crackling logs.

John's sudden voice in her ear made her jump. 'Penny for your thoughts,' he offered.

Amie stretched out her arms and yawned. 'My thoughts were far away,' she answered.

John extricated himself from the armchair and switched on the radio. 'How about a smooch to dance music?' he asked.

The young woman glanced up at him and giggled. 'Sounds good,' she agreed.

John found a station playing old songs and took Amie in his arms. They danced, though hardly moving, her head on his shoulder and his cheek against her hair. All the sentimental old favourites floated like spectres in the air, tugging at the heartstrings. Everything seemed so sad.

Amie wanted to ask John for reassurance about his relationship with Joanne Webber. Was this really a business relationship or was she sincere? Why had she confronted Amie and told her to stay away? John became so angry when she questioned him, that she hesitated to bring the subject up while they were so happy together.

Amie brushed shameful tears from her eyes and broke away from John. 'I fancy a cup of coffee,' she said.

John looked taken aback. 'My mind was far away this time, dreaming of exotic trips with you,' he confessed.

This pleased Amie but she went to make the hot drink, needing a clear head. They drank their coffee, then went to bed, to lie there intimately entwined. The night sky outside the bedroom window was like black velvet, studded with ice-bright stars as sharp as diamonds. Hooting and screeching from nocturnal birds and animals drifted in from the distance.

Amie lay against John's back, with her arms round him. His breathing was regular and heavy as he slept soundly. Holding him tight would not keep him with her forever. Unbidden tears trickled down her cheeks as she wished the night would go on and on.

The silver crescent moon appeared in the frame of the window, slowly described an arc across the blackness of the sky, and disappeared from sight. Amie closed her eyes and drifted into fitful slumber. The sleeping young woman did not see the gradual grey tinge appearing in the sky. Nor did she hear the first solitary call of a bird pierce the morning sky.

Chapter Fourteen

'Wake up, sleepy head,' called John's voice in Amie's ear. There was the smell of frying bacon and fresh coffee; blue sky showed in the window frame.

'Are you always so lively in the morning?' mumbled Amie.

'Nine o'clock already, and yes, I'll show you how lively!' responded John.

'Get away!' shrieked Amie, as the weight of the man pinned her to the bed.

This was to no avail, as John pulled off his shirt and slacks to slip into the bed. His cold hands wandered rapidly over her body, bringing a response of desire to her. Their lips met in a long kiss as if they would never part. His body pressed insistently against hers as he became aroused and urgently made love to her.

As John lay exhausted afterwards, he became aware of the breakfast threatening to spoil. He leapt from the bed and turned off the cooker, serving the breakfast naked. With a tray on her knees, Amie sat up, watching her lover seated on the bed with his coffee cup between his two hands to warm them. There was a feeling of anticlimax, as she would have liked to cuddle for a while after making love.

'Come back to bed for a few minutes,' entreated Amie.

'Why, you're just a little flirt,' teased John.

Amie pushed the tray away from her and lay down, pulling the covers up to her chin. John picked the tray up and went into the kitchen. He returned and, pulling back the covers, slipped into bed with her. His rough chin brushed her cheek as he embraced her.

'Is this what you want?' he whispered hoarsely in her ear.

'Oh yes,' she answered.

'Women usually do, I guess,' he remarked, spoiling the moment.

Amie tried not to betray her hurt by tensing her body. Nestled in the curve of his body, she made herself relax, knowing that John would be annoyed if she made a fuss about her feelings.

'We meet and make love', murmured Amie, 'yet we never seem to talk much. I want to know more about you.'

John laughed. 'Nothing much to say. I'm just a good-natured guy looking for a good time.'

Amie objected. 'No, I need to know what you were like as a child and how you became what you are now.'

'I was just a kid with an elder brother and decent parents,' John replied. 'We played in the yard, went to junior and high school and college, dated a few girls and I came out here to study and get work where the money is. Luckily I had connections. That is, Dad had business connections to help me get started.'

'Why did Robert James leave England and come to work here?' Amie asked. 'All his ties must have been there.'

'Well', said John, 'since you want to know, he wanted to get away after his wife, Veronica, and children – you know. His parents suggested he came back with me to recover. He was depressed and needed a change. As I needed a partner in my business and he is a clever man, he came back with me and has been here for a couple of years.' He coughed gruffly to hide his feelings.

'So,' said Amie, 'you are an old softie, after all.'

'We lost my kid sister through illness a few years ago,' confessed John. 'So I know how he feels.'

'I'm sorry,' consoled Amie. 'I didn't know you had a sister.'

'Come on, we have to go,' said John briskly, swinging his legs out of the bed and reaching for his clothes.

What was left of the morning was spent in dressing for travelling and tidying the cabin ready for leaving. The blue sky had been overtaken by black clouds and soon a steady drizzle of rain was falling in a monotonous pitter-patter on the cabin roof.

'We can't take a stroll in this weather,' said John. 'Would you like a snack before we travel back down?'

'Yes, fine,' agreed Amie.

John seemed remote and preoccupied about going back to his work. He said he had to get back for some business calls. Soon they were ready to go down, yet the evening was already hovering in the wings.

Is the pleasure we had in this place worth the sadness of leaving? Amie demanded silently of herself. John did not seem to care and was quite eager to leave.

Sandwiches and coffee in the early afternoon staved off the pangs of hunger for the downward journey. The two lovers left the cabin soon after this. The drive was hazardous. The drizzle had evolved into unusually heavy rain.

'We should have left earlier,' said John. 'This trail is turning to mud.'

Sure enough, the road was sodden, with little streams of water busily running downhill. The car needed to be driven slowly and carefully. The rain tapped insistently on the windscreen. With rhythmic movements, the windscreen wipers whooshed away the constantly re-forming layers of water.

Halfway down, the edge of the track gave way at a sharp, rain-eroded turn, plunging the car, together with the unfortunate occupants, down the hill.

'Look out!' screamed Amie, too late.

Their wild career downhill was abruptly halted by a solid, broad and immovable old tree. The car shuddered, scattering broken glass onto the mud. The wheels rested on crushed bushes. Still the rain came down in sheets like an impenetrable fog.

John lay, immobile, across the steering wheel. A line of blood trickled down his face. Amie was conscious, lying back, but too shocked to move. For a long time nothing stirred.

The rain was gushing down the windows. Drips were coming through on to the back seat were the roof was gashed. Slowly, she moved one arm at a time, then her feet and legs. When she tried to lift her head, this proved to be impossible.

Amie did not panic. The young woman felt an unusual calmness and acceptance. The tree would prevent the car from moving farther down the hill. Someone would be sure to find them sooner or later.

As time went by the light began to dim. *Must be night-time. The rain is getting darker,* thought Amie to herself. This struck her as funny and she began to giggle. A sharp pain brought her laughter to a stop and she realised that to move her neck might be dangerous.

John had not moved, although Amie could hear him breathing raggedly. Stretching out her left hand, she felt his knee and leg. He was cold but nothing seemed to be broken. His arm and back felt fine as far as she could tell.

John began to groan: at least he was regaining consciousness. He raised his right hand to his head. His fingers, already bloody, collected more blood from his temple.

Cautiously, John lifted his head and gingerly raised himself from the steering wheel. He felt his face with trembling hands. Taking a packet of tissues from the glove compartment, he wiped his face.

'Goddammit!' he muttered. 'Amie, are you all right?'

'Get me some help, John,' she pleaded, but there was silence. He had lost consciousness again.

Amie sat there, unable to move, watching the night go by and slowly become the day. Suppose no one found them! The dawn had arrived, although darkness still prevailed in the gully, when she heard the distant sound of voices calling. There was a prolonged scrabbling noise, a torch shone in her window and the wonderful face of Robert James peered anxiously in.

Chapter Fifteen

Amie began to sob, helplessly, as Robert James forced open the car door on her side.

'Water,' Amie murmured through parched lips.

Robert put a flask to her mouth to moisten her lips. 'Try not to swallow. You might need an operation,' he cautioned.

'Okay,' agreed Amie, allowing herself to sink into oblivion.

As a helicopter hovered overhead like an irate dragonfly, more rescuers descended by ropes to the car. A medical team examined the two trapped passengers and extracted them, still unconscious, from the car. Fortunately, the rain gradually ceased from then on, making the rescue work easier. An ambulance, conveying the two patients and several cars made their way gingerly down the remaining route to safety.

Amie awoke to inert consciousness in a hospital room. All was quiet and white. Raising her hand to her neck, she felt a bulky collar rendering her head immobile. There was a throbbing pain in her temples.

As she groaned, her mother's face appeared in view. 'Oh baby, just you lie there and don't try to move,' Rose urged softly.

The older woman placed a damp cloth on her daughter's aching brow.

'Amie do you remember what happened?' Rose asked her in a gentle voice. 'You are in hospital.'

'Yes, I remember the crash,' said Amie, quietly. 'Give me a drink would you, Mom.'

Rose held a plastic bottle with a straw to Amie's lips. 'The nurse said you must just have a sip,' she cautioned.

Amie felt the cool liquid refreshing her dry mouth and sighed. Rose told Amie that John was in the same hospital and not in any danger. Poppy sent her love and would be visiting in the morning. The office had been informed of the accident. There was no need to worry about anything.

Tears ran down Amie's cheeks. 'I'm sorry, Mom,' she sobbed. 'I have caused you too much trouble.'

'Hush,' soothed Rose. 'The anaesthetic has upset you. Just get yourself well.'

At that point a doctor and nurse entered the room, so Rose left to go home. The doctor was silver-haired and elderly. He spoke to Amie as if to a child but she was too exhausted to care. The sun cast mocking rays at her through the slats of the venetian blinds at the window.

'So, young lady, you are back with us,' remarked the doctor as he listened to Amie's heart. 'Yes, that's fine. The nurse is going to take your blood pressure. That collar must stay on your neck for the time being – and the cast, of course.'

So saying, he swept smartly out of the room. The nurse, a small woman of oriental origin, began to tend Amie. Having tidied the bed, the nurse placed a vase of flowers on a table where her patient could see them. For the first time, Amie realised her left arm was in a plaster cast.

'Nurse,' Amie called out sharply, 'Is there anything else wrong with me? No one tells me anything.'

The Chinese girl smiled sweetly. 'You have an injured neck and must remain immobile until the doctor says you can move. Also one fractured arm. You have had operations since you had the car crash and have been here two days. Your mother was very worried when you were slow to come round but now you must rest.'

'Two days!' exclaimed Amie. 'I didn't know. How is the man I was with?'

'I do not know,' replied the nurse. 'I find out for you.'

Smiling with an efficient nod, the nurse left the room. Amie began to sit up, then remembered she must not move. There was a good view of the ceiling, and of the flowers if she looked from the corners of her eyes. Then the dim memory of a man's face looking anxiously at her through the car window came back to her.

The nurse re-entered the room. 'Mr John Peters is in another room. He had concussion and bruising. His left wrist is broken and right knee strained. Nothing serious,' she said.

'Oh,' sighed Amie, feeling sorry for John. Then, thinking about herself, 'Nurse, can't I sit up more? I hate lying on my back not seeing anything. Also I need something for my headache.'

'I have to ask the doctor first,' replied the nurse. 'First I give you something to make you sleep and then you must have food.'

The nurse gave Amie an injection in her right arm, waited until her patient's regular breathing showed she was in a healthy sleep and rustled from the room. The sun sank slowly past the window, giving a last golden glimmer through the slats of the venetian blind. The evening and night drew a mantle of rest over the wards and rooms. If only the unusually heavy rain had held off a few days ago, the accident would never have happened!

Amie gradually regained consciousness the next morning and saw a much-loved face looking anxiously down at her.

'Mommy,' cried Poppy, hugging her mother and kissing her cheek. 'Does your arm hurt very much?'

Amie had to laugh, in spite of everything. 'Not as much as my neck, and that's a lot,' she answered. 'I'm so happy to see you. Are you all right? I hope you are being good for Grandma.'

'Of course I am,' Poppy replied indignantly, tossing her auburn curls.

'My little redhead girl,' whispered Amie, embracing her daughter with her good right arm.

'Of course she has been good,' came Rose's voice. 'I said I would bring her to see you.'

'Thank you,' replied Amie. 'I am cheered up just to see her. By the way I can't see who is in here, lying flat on my back.'

'Here comes the nurse. We can see you later,' said Rose.

The Chinese nurse came in to look after Amie. At last the head of the bed was raised to give her a better view. The nurse bathed her patient's face and hands to refresh her. A little light breakfast renewed her energy.

Poppy came bouncing back in and thrust a home-made get well card and a bright pink flower in a pot at her mother.

'Darling, how sweet of you,' laughed Amie. 'You are better than any tonic.'

Poppy placed the card and flower on the bedside table, where Amie could see them.

'Were the flowers from you?' Amie asked her mother, who had followed Poppy into the room.

'Yes, dear,' replied Rose. 'I wanted something pretty for you to look at when you awoke. How are you now?'

'Not so woozy, but everything hurts. Even my legs ache, although I can wiggle my toes so they must be intact.' responded Amie.

'That must be the bruising. You'll settle down, soon enough,' comforted Rose.

Poppy was given time off from school to visit her mother. This made the experience even more of a treat for her. After a while the grandmother and granddaughter went home, promising to return the next day. The nurse brought Amie a light lunch, instructing her to have a nap afterwards.

Suddenly, Amie was rudely awakened from her doze by the sound of the door crashing open. A woman stood framed in the doorway. Honey blonde hair was drawn back in a chignon. The slim lines of her figure were hugged by a grey pin-striped tailored suit.

Chapter Sixteen

For a moment, Amie wondered where she was. Could this be part of the nightmare of the car accident she had been reliving in her sleep? Certainly the shock of the sudden awakening made her jump nervously and want to hide away. Instead, she had to lie there, helpless, on her hospital bed.

The woman, having closed the door quietly but firmly, advanced briskly to the side of the bed. Amie dismissed the last vestiges of sleep from her mind and looked sternly at her visitor.

'I'm sorry,' said Amie. 'This is a private room. You must have the wrong room.'

'I don't think so,' retorted the woman. 'I came to see you, Mrs Blake.'

Amie immediately recognised the voice of the woman. Of course, the cut glass tones from the phone, Joanne Webber! What in heaven's name was she doing here? This was all a bad dream!

Amie put her hand to her head as the room swam around her.

'I know that voice, Miss Joanne Webber,' Amie replied, sharply. 'Look, I am ill and would like a little peace and quiet.'

'Not until I have had my say,' Joanne answered, in equally acerbic tones. 'You may well lie there looking pale and interesting but you don't cut any ice with me. There aren't any men here now to be taken in by cheap little tarts like you. John has told me all about how you made him spend the weekend with you, with your blackmailing ways.'

'You begged him to meet you for one last time or you would make things difficult for him,' she continued. 'Well, I am here to tell you I can make things very difficult for you. Stop chasing my fiancé now or you'll be extremely sorry. My father is a powerful man with great influence.'

'I have never chased anyone in my life,' interjected Amie. 'John was the one who pursued me. Your relationship was only business, or so I am told. *We* are really close.'

'Trust you to think that one up,' scoffed Joanne. 'I am sure John would never say that. He is devoted to me. Also I would not be surprised if you had arranged that little car crash to tie him to you more securely.'

'That's a crazy thing to say,' interrupted Amie. 'You are full of lies!'

'He has not come running in to see you yet, has he?' demanded Joanne, triumphantly, her voice becoming harsher every moment she spoke. 'You think you look so glamorous, lying there in white, your hair all over the pillow. Save your looks for some other fool. John has asked my forgiveness and has promised not to be taken in by you ever again.'

'I don't believe this,' gasped Amie, raising her hand to her forehead. 'I want you to leave me alone.'

'We shall both leave you alone,' said Joanne, crisply, gaining control of her emotions. 'You have caused enough trouble. Stay at home and look after your child. I hear you already have one failed marriage, so don't try to spoil mine!'

The little Chinese nurse, Daisy, hurried into the room. 'So sorry, Mrs Blake', she said, 'are you all right?'

'This lady is just leaving,' said Amie, relieved to see the nurse.

'Forgive my intrusion, nurse,' said Joanne. 'I must have entered the wrong room.'

Joanne walked out coolly, and calmly shut the door behind her.

Daisy fussed round Amie. 'You should have rung for me,' she scolded. 'I could hear raised voices way down the corridor.'

'Just a misunderstanding, I think,' said Amie, feeling the tears beginning to roll down her cheeks.

Daisy took Amie in her arms and hugged her. 'Never mind Mrs Blake, that woman should not have shouted at you. The doctor must examine you now and you must not be upset.'

Amie realised that the argument had been heard all over the hospital. How embarrassing! What on earth had made her get into such a mess? John could not have made those remarks about her to Joanne!

The silver-haired Doctor Mason was summoned by Daisy. He found Amie in a helpless, weepy state. Nothing seemed to matter any more. While Amie had been fluttering about, like a butterfly in blossoms, Joanne had been investigating her and digging into her past.

'Come along, little lady,' soothed Doctor Mason. He injected a sedative into Amie's right arm. As she drifted away into unconsciousness, Amie could hear Doctor Mason's voice scolding Daisy: 'Remember to keep everyone out of this room except the mother and the daughter. Mrs Blake needs lots of rest.'

Next day, Amie awoke to find Poppy waiting by her bedside. The little girl jumped up from the chair and kissed her mother.

'That nurse, you know she has a flower name, just like me,' remarked Poppy. 'Well, she said we have to be really quiet today because you are sick. Shall I read to you? I can sit here and read to myself if you like.'

'What about your school?' asked Amie, frowning. 'You must not miss any more classes.'

'Silly,' replied Poppy. 'This is the weekend! You have lost track of the time.'

Daisy entered the room and beamed at Poppy. 'This lady makes you happy?' she queried.

'Of course,' agreed Amie. 'Is my mother here?'

'I fetch her for you,' said Daisy, leaving the room.

Rose bustled into the room. 'I thought you would like to see Poppy on her own,' she said. 'By the way, someone left you a card at the reception desk.'

Amie took the sealed envelope from her mother. Opening the envelope, she took out a beautiful card decorated with red roses and pink satin ribbons. Inside was a printed message: *With My Sincere Wishes For Your Speedy Recovery*. Written on the blank page was:

Dear Amie, I am so sorry how events turned out for you. There seems no reason for me to remain here, so I am returning to England. Forgive me for not visiting you in hospital. I thought this was for the best, so wishing you a happy future life,
Yours ever, Robert James

Amie gazed, stupefied, at the message on the card. So Robert James was leaving her too. Now she felt strangely alone. He seemed to have always been there in the background, a bit of a nuisance, but now he was leaving a gap in her life.

'Who was that from?' intruded Poppy's voice, startling Amie.

'Someone I used to know,' said Amie.

'Not that John Peters!' exclaimed Rose.

'No, not him; someone else,' replied Amie, sadly.

'Shall I put that with your other cards?' asked Poppy.

'No, there are too many there already,' said Amie, putting the card back into the envelope. Strangely, she did not want anyone else to see the message.

Amie looked round at the room. There were cards from the girls at work, flowers, pot plants and even one of those silly star-shaped balloons, depicting a bear's face and flaunting the legend *Get Well Soon My Hunny*, from her ex-husband, Derek Blake, in the room. Trust him to make a silly joke out of everything. He hated to be serious and that had been their trouble.

Amie forced a smile. 'I think we have enough cards up without any more,' she told Poppy. 'Mother, I want to go home,' she said, turning to Rose, who knew when her daughter called her 'mother' she was serious.

Chapter Seventeen

Amie was persuaded to remain in hospital for a few more days while she built up her strength. Determined to escape from that place of torture, she obeyed orders, ate her meals and exercised her legs to help retain their circulation. Soon she was able to walk round her room, feeling weak and dizzy at first. Regaining her confidence, she was then promoted to the day room, watching television with sundry other convalescents or looking through the french windows at the lush lawns and brilliant blooms in the spacious grounds of the hospital. Eventually she could even sit outside although only for short periods of time and in a wheelchair.

Amie had a secret plan. There was no way she could leave without speaking to John. Just because Joanne had paid her spiteful visit and spilt her poisonous remarks into the atmosphere, there was no reason to believe that John had condoned her actions. As soon as there was a chance, Amie would make her way to his room to ask what was happening.

At this point an orderly brought a note from John. Put simply, the gist was that he would like to see her. There was something they must discuss. Immediately, the nagging anxiety lifted from the pit of Amie's stomach and in a split second, her mood changed from misery to wild, thumping, churning, extravagant excitement.

Now she would not have to enter his room in a nervous condition. Everything would be all right. A weight had been lifted from her shoulders. At last they would be together again.

That afternoon, Amie carefully combed her hair into waves and applied lipstick to her neglected lips. Dressed in her prettiest cream coloured night-gown and daffodil yellow robe, she set off down the corridor to visit her lover. They had not met for so long: she had lost track of time in that place. The collar was still on her neck; her left arm was encased in plaster, various cuts and bruises were bandaged and her right ankle was strapped due to a sprain, discovered when she first attempted to walk again.

Amie set off to visit John. When she arrived at his door, she knocked timorously. The door was opened by a nurse, who stood back to admit the visitor, then left them alone. The two of them, one standing by the door and the other seated in a wheelchair by the window, looked guardedly at each other.

There was a long pause. Amie approached John, who was wearing light blue pyjamas and a dark navy robe, taking in the scar on his face, the left arm in a sling and both legs in plaster.

'You seem to have worse injuries than they said John,' blurted out Amie. 'No wonder you didn't contact me before.'

'I have been confused,' agreed John. 'I had a knock on the head; but you look great in those colours!'

Amie crossed the room and seated herself on the chair next to him. Leaning forward, she kissed John's mouth, gently. Strangely, he did not respond. He must be feeling ill.

John coughed and began to speak gruffly. 'Amie, I could not contact you before but now I am out of bed we must get this straight. We can't go on. This accident has brought everything out. You are a swell babe, but now that Joanne has found out we have to finish.'

Amie stared at him in disbelief. 'What!' she exclaimed. 'I don't understand. You can't mean this. You mean not to meet again? I thought we were in love.'

John flushed an embarrassed red. 'Look,' he replied, 'we had a great time but I promised you nothing. You must see I am marrying the girl and have to keep her sweet. The matter of business comes into this. The family is influential and that comes before a bit of fun, even with a gorgeous chick like you.'

Amie felt paralysed with shock. 'Did you know that Joanne woman came into my room and shouted at me when I was lying there in pain on the second day here? At the time I thought she was just being bitchy – but apparently you had sent her! Were you too much of a coward to do the dirty deed yourself? Don't forget you were driving the car that injured me.'

'Come on, don't start all that,' remonstrated John.

'What I mean is, have you heard of adding insult to injury?' explained Amie.

'Oh darling', said John, turning on the charm, 'I didn't send Joanne in to see you. Work it out for yourself. If that happened on the second day, I was out of this world. There was no way I could have even spoken to anyone or thought anything out. I was in and out of consciousness most of the time.'

Immediately Amie felt a pang of guilt. 'I'm sorry. Perhaps we can leave this for a bit and talk later, when we feel better.'

'Look, sweetheart,' said John. 'Joanne should never have done that to you. That girl is lovely but she has a mean streak. We have to give up for now. Things are too dodgy. Perhaps later when everyone has calmed down we can get together again.'

'I don't believe this!' gasped Amie in disbelief. 'You surely don't think I would share you with her. Apparently you intend to marry the bitch! How can you treat me like this? I thought we were a couple, and you want me to be your slut, your whore, to visit in your spare time.'

The joy of hearing John call her sweetheart had clashed with the awfulness of hearing him speak of Joanne as his partner, and this nearly drove Amie wild.

'Of course I am going to marry Joanne,' said John unfazed. 'I never said I wasn't. Put this all down to experience. We had a good time. I enjoyed myself – and I know you did, you little sexpot – so why not be friends and remember those nights on the rug in the cabin?'

'You're despicable,' Amie spluttered. 'You make me feel dirty! I would never have met you like that if I had known. Now I remember, you were always evasive and would not answer any questions about you and her. I feel used and degraded.'

Amie stood up and left the room without looking back at the man she had thought was her future. Feeling strangely numb, she made her way back to her room. The rest of the afternoon she spent gazing miserably through the window at the no longer uplifting bushes and flowers. When her mother and daughter arrived for their evening visit, Amie reintroduced her plan to leave hospital.

'I am sure I am well enough to return home,' Amie whispered sadly. 'You must take me out of here.'

'Fine by me, dear,' Rose responded. 'I would be relieved not to have this journey every day; not that I minded visiting you.' The older woman hastened to reassure her daughter.

'No, you have been wonderful,' Amie replied. 'What would I have done without you?'

'I'll speak to the doctor,' Rose answered, 'don't worry.' The two women hugged each other before parting.

Poppy, too, was eager to see her mother come home. Rose spoke to Doctor Mason. He agreed, saying that Amie was becoming depressed and perhaps needed her home comforts to lessen her moodiness. At last the day came for the family to be reunited.

Rose brought in some clothes for Amie to wear on the way home. Outside clothing felt strange after wearing night attire for so long. The little nurse, Daisy, was pleased with the gift of perfume for all her care. Poppy excitedly held her mother's arm as they emerged slowly from the hospital room into the corridor on their way out.

There the little group saw a woman pushing a man in a wheelchair towards them. The man was John Peters and the woman was Joanne Webber. There was hardly a pause as the two parties passed each other. However emotions ran high in some of the participants.

To Amie, the scene was frozen in time. Hoping to leave the hospital without having to face John again, not only had she been confronted by him, but also by the woman who was to marry him. Appearing calm was difficult. Getting out of there seemed to take forever, but at last they were through the doors and driving home in their car.

Chapter Eighteen

Later on that day, Rose made a phone call to her friend, George Lestrange. The idea had been to meet him for a drink that evening.

'Hello, George,' said Rose when she got through to him.

'Hello, darling,' said George in a pleased voice.

'Look, Amie came out of hospital this morning,' explained Rose. 'Anyway I'm not too pleased with her condition.'

'Why, what's wrong with her?' asked George. 'I thought she was passed fit to leave there.'

Rose gazed through the kitchen window as she absentmindedly twisted her apron string around her finger. Poppy was playing outside, riding round on her bicycle. The little girl was rapidly growing out of her clothes. Strange how quickly time passed and children grew up!

'Something is wrong, George,' continued Rose. 'All the fight seems to have gone out of Amie and she just lies there, looking through the window at the trees.'

'I understand,' soothed George. 'Forget about tonight. You need to be with her.'

'I am sorry about this George.' Rose rubbed her weary brow with her free hand. 'I very much wanted to see you.'

'I love you, darling.' George's voice deepened even more with emotion. 'See you soon and we'll make up for lost time.'

Rose put down the receiver and turned to go up the stairs. As she neared Amie's room, she could hear the sound of gentle sobbing. This was not a grieving noise of unhappiness. No, her daughter was crying as naturally as she was breathing; the tears running monotonous and unchecked down her cheeks as she gazed vacantly out at the sky.

Rose had to call in the doctor after a while. Amie was unwilling to eat, drink, talk or get out of bed. All she wanted to do was lie there, sobbing. Nothing else seemed to matter.

Even little Poppy could do nothing to raise her spirits. The doctor examined Amie. He could find no inflammation in her injuries. There was only one conclusion.

'This woman is having a nervous breakdown,' Doctor Schwartz told Rose. 'Something else, apart from the car accident, has happened to her to cause this.'

'There was a man she was seeing,' ventured Rose. 'I wonder whether he had anything to do with this...'

'We'll have to get her back into hospital, quickly,' Doctor Schwartz decided. 'Pack a bag for her.'

'Oh dear,' Rose wiped a tear from her own eye. 'Poor Amie, she does seem to attract trouble.'

Amie was whisked back into hospital. There she lay in deep depression as her wounds healed, but not her mind. Rose kept Poppy away from her mother as the child would have been upset by the lack of response. Derek Blake, Amie's ex-husband, was informed and came to visit his former wife.

His response was bafflement. He was always cheerful himself and could not understand this sort of thing. The reception he got was total blankness. This woman, the mother of his child, would not speak or even look at him, so he could not tell her to pull herself together!

As the school holidays were on, Poppy went away with her father and his new wife for a vacation. The second Mrs

Blake was a slightly plump, but pretty, fluffy-haired blonde called Myrna. As Derek was in real estate, he had no difficulty in renting a cottage for a couple of weeks. The child was thoroughly spoiled and pampered, which did her no harm at all.

Rose was left alone in the house she had shared with her daughter and granddaughter. The place seemed quiet and empty without them. However, now was the opportunity for a good turnout and spring clean. That would distract her from her worries for Amie.

As Rose was sorting out her washing, the morning after Poppy had left to go on vacation with her father and his new wife, there was a ring at the front door. Wanda Merrington was standing there, a silly little veiled hat perched on her head and a smart navy suit clinging to her hips. Her eyes took in Rose's appearance. An eyebrow was raised.

'I see you are busy being the hausfrau,' commented Wanda tartly. 'Just popped round for a moment. We were passing and I wondered how Amie was. When are we going to see you at the tea dance?'

'Wanda, I was doing the washing,' Rose said, explaining her appearance, and smoothing down her apron. 'Won't you come in for coffee?'

'No thank you, dear,' gushed Wanda, nodding towards the car waiting outside for her. 'Fred and I are out on a date; off to see his relatives.'

'This is getting serious,' smiled Rose. 'I'm so happy for you.'

Wanda winked and trotted off down the path as Fred tooted the car horn at her. Rose couldn't help smiling at her friend's infectious gaiety. As she filled the washing machine with bed linen, her thoughts wandered to the man she loved. On an impulse, she walked to the phone and dialled George's number.

His familiar deep voice answered immediately. 'I knew you were on the line,' he enthused. 'I was thinking of ringing you myself.'

Rose felt happier to hear his voice. 'I wondered how you were,' she replied. 'What have you been doing these past few days?'

'I was just on the point of leaving,' said George. 'I am playing golf with old Ben this afternoon, but I can cancel if you want to see me.'

'No, you go ahead and enjoy yourself,' protested Rose. 'Why don't you come here this evening and I'll cook you dinner, as I'm alone at the moment.'

George thought this was a good idea and promised to be there at six with a bottle. Rose explained about Amie being in hospital and Poppy away with her father. The rest of the day was happier, with the plans for the dinner to be considered. First the hospital needed to be contacted, but the patient was no better.

George, looking smart in a dark suit, arrived promptly at six that evening. Rose wore her white linen full-skirted gown to greet him at the door. A gold chain glittered at her throat. The red belt at her waist added a touch of colour.

George stepped into the hallway and quickly closed the door behind him. 'Darling, I missed you,' he murmured, taking her gently in his arms. 'Why, you look just like a bride!'

Rose laughed. 'Come and sit down,' she suggested, leading him by the hand into the living room. 'I missed you too, my love.'

George stopped her in the doorway and embraced her. 'Let's get married,' he begged. 'I've waited long enough.'

Rose snuggled into his shoulder. 'That would be wonderful,' she agreed. 'But I can't at the moment as Amie has had a nervous breakdown and all I can think of is her.'

Becoming more serious, George took Rose's hand and sat with her on the sofa. 'That's terrible!' he exclaimed. 'I wondered how she was, but this...' He paused.

Smoothing back her hair, Rose sighed. 'That is why I am alone. They had to take her back into hospital and Poppy has gone to stay with her father for a few days.'

'You are having a rough time, but nice for me,' said George. 'I have you all to myself. And what is that succulent smell?'

Chapter Nineteen

'I must get back to the kitchen,' declared Rose firmly. 'Where is the bottle you promised me?'

George had left the wine outside. He hurried out to the car. When he re-entered the house he was carrying the bottle. Also cradled in his hands was a bouquet of red roses.

They drank to each other with champagne. Candlelight gleamed on the crystal glasses. Music surrounded them as they sat at the lace-covered table. The steak was tender, the crispy potatoes just right with sweetcorn and peas.

When the meal was finished, George leaned towards Rose. He held her hand across the table and slipped a sapphire ring on to her finger.

'Rose, say you are bound to me,' pleaded George. 'Marry me!'

'Of course I shall,' soothed Rose. 'I must wait until Amie is better and then nothing shall stop us.'

George squeezed her hand. Rose got to her feet and drew him to the kitchen. The floor there was smoother for dancing. They moved in unison slowly round the room, swaying to the music.

'Do you like the ring?' asked George.

'George, I love my ring,' answered Rose and kissed him, and then they stopped dancing.

They walked, hand in hand, to the stairway. For once Rose had the house to herself. We each need to think about ourselves for a change. Looking after her family had left her little time to be with George.

Now they walked up the stairs, arm in arm. 'Am I staying the night?' asked George.

The slim woman looked up at him, mischievously. 'If you're sure I won't compromise you,' responded Rose, pinching his arm.

When George awoke the next morning, Rose was not in the bed. He dressed hurriedly and padded down the stairs in his socks. There were clattering sounds from the kitchen. Wearing her night-gown and robe, his companion was clearing up the kitchen.

George walked quietly behind Rose and wrapped his arms around her waist. 'I thought you had left me until I remembered this was your house,' he said, kissing her ear.

Rose tried to turn her head to look at George. 'You startled me as I couldn't hear you. We left this place in a mess last night,' she tried to sound stern.

'What a wonderful night,' sighed George. 'We aren't bad for a couple of old folks; well, I am old anyway.'

'You are all I want', reassured Rose, 'my comfort and life.'

George turned her round to face him and they hugged each other. Rose clasped George to her tightly. For so long she had been alone. Now a wonderful man had come into her life; someone of flesh and blood to love and cherish her.

Then the phone rang. Derek was on the line to enquire after Amie. After that, Terrie from the office rang with her best wishes. Reluctantly, Rose let go of George and got on with the business of the day.

Rose made coffee and toast. George shaved and had to leave, promising to phone later on in the day. Amie's friend, Betty, who had been out of town and had only just heard about the accident, rang with messages of concern.

Wanda called to report on her meeting with her in-laws-to-be yesterday.

Rose said nothing to any of them about the events of last night, only that she and George had a pleasant evening together. Smiling as she worked, cleaning was no chore as she happily cleared up the dinner dishes from the previous evening. While in the mood, she washed the kitchen floor. There was no shopping or washing to do.

Rose suddenly realised she was still wearing her night-gown and robe. Scolding herself under her breath, she hurried upstairs to shower and change. Donning a sweater and slacks, she made herself ready for her daily visit to the hospital. As she looked into the other two bedrooms on her way downstairs, she thought how sad the two beds looked, turned down and waiting for their occupants.

A large pink elephant, named Juno, lay patiently on Amie's pillow, and Old Ted glowered from Poppy's bedside table as usual. As Rose drove towards the hospital, she thought to herself that the girls were like two babies for her to look after. If only they would grow up! Arriving at the car park, she hurried into the building.

Amie was improving, so she was told. Certainly she was sitting up in a chair in her room and the weeping had ceased. The young woman's face was pale and drawn. Rose sat in the chair next to her and took her daughter's limp hand in her own.

'How are you feeling?' Rose asked.

'So tired, my legs are weak,' Amie muttered.

'You need to build your strength up,' advised Rose. 'You need some chicken noodle soup and scrambled eggs.'

'I shall eat something,' agreed Amie. 'Soon I'll be back at work.'

Rose doubted that but said nothing. What Amie needed was a long, restful holiday. Something had to be done.

They had some money but not really enough to spend on trips abroad.

After her visit, Rose spoke to Doctor Mason, who had not wanted his patient to leave hospital so soon on the previous occasion. He considered that Amie needed lots of rest and quiet. When he decided she could go home there must be nothing to disturb or upset her. Meanwhile she must remain in her hospital room, neither exerting herself in any way, nor being agitated by well-meaning visitors, except her mother of course.

Rose drove thoughtfully home. Everything was heaped on her shoulders again. What she needed was a break. Perhaps George could help.

When Rose arrived home, she phoned George. 'I am so tired, I need a rest. Can't we go to the beach?'

The reply was comforting. 'Of course, I have some consultancy work to do this afternoon. Is tomorrow all right?'

Although George was retired, he still acted as a part-time consultant. He was highly regarded in his circle.

'Fine, I'll make up a picnic basket,' said Rose. 'George, I have to talk to you about something.'

'Sounds interesting,' said George. 'Is anyone else coming with us?'

Rose said she would ask her friend Wanda. The party was sure to be jolly with her along. Wanda agreed enthusiastically and eagerly phoned Fred to invite him to join the party. George would ferry everyone down to the beach, so all was set.

Rose did not see George that night. However she was surprised by a visit from Betty Steiner. This lady swept into the house in a wave of perfume. The outfit she wore was cheerful, consisting of a red top and black skirt, with patent handbag and stiletto shoes.

Balancing herself on the edge of an armchair, Betty accepted a cup of coffee from Rose. 'Honestly, I didn't know anything about the accident until I got back. I've been back to see Mom and Dad and there's a boy there I used to know. We got acquainted again. I kinda feel responsible for what happened to Amie.'

'Oh surely not, dear,' interrupted Rose.

'I introduced her to that rat John Peters. If I hadn't she would never have been in that car with him. He made a play for her straightaway. I warned her to keep away from that heel, and now look what has happened.'

'You're so kind to Amie but she is a grown woman and must make her own decisions,' said Rose.

Thinking of the events of the past few weeks, Rose said goodbye to her guest, promising to keep her informed of Amie's progress. Now she had to get ready for her afternoon of relaxation in the sun with her friends.

Chapter Twenty

Rose gathered together her swimsuit and giant towel. The sandwiches for the hamper were soon ready. Drinks, fresh fruit, condiments and serviettes completed the picnic. Sunglasses and oil were other essentials for an afternoon in the sun.

George arrived, wearing a short-sleeved shirt and slacks. He kissed his fiancée tenderly, before carrying the hamper out to his car. Rose slid into the passenger seat, placing the big straw bag containing her beach things by her feet. The warmth of the early afternoon sun was reflected from the road.

'You're not wearing your ring!' exclaimed George as they drove off to collect Wanda and Fred.

'Honestly, I can't wear that on the beach,' retorted Rose.

'Are you ashamed of me?' asked George.

'Don't be silly, I don't want to lose my lovely ring, and the size needs adjusting,' explained Rose.

Soon the exuberant Wanda and jolly Fred were ensconced in the back seats of the car and the party made their way to the beach. They looked forward to a restful afternoon.

As they stretched out on their row of loungers, the quartet laughed and joked. Rose removed her lavender cotton sundress to reveal a pale blue swimsuit. George leaned towards her from his lounger to apply sun oil to her back. 'You look like a goddess,' he told her quietly.

Rose nodded appreciatively and tied a purple patterned cotton square round her head to protect her hair from the sun. Wanda adjusted her black reinforced swimsuit to show off her plump figure to the best advantage.

'Being blonde,' she confided in Rose. 'Dark colours set off my complexion.' Her friend smiled, knowing her true hair colour came from a bottle.

Rose sighed and glanced at George. 'I wish Amie could be here to enjoy herself with us.'

He shrugged and carried on reading his paper. 'Give her time and plenty of rest.'

'I want her to come home to be looked after by me,' said Rose, scooping up sand with one hand and watching the fine stream of grains drift down again in a neat heap. 'When she is strong enough I want to take her to Europe for a vacation.'

'These are great plans!' agreed George.

Fred heaved himself to his feet, patting his protuberant belly. 'Come along, girls,' he wheezed. 'I need some exercise.'

Wanda jumped up and took his hand. 'Rose, let's go swim,' she called out looking back over her shoulder at her friend.

Rose declined for the time being but encouraged George to go with the others, saying someone had to look after their possessions. The tall, thin man set off down the beach in pursuit of the two overweight friends. Fred and Wanda were already halfway to the sea, holding hands and running carefully but steadily.

Rose lay on her lounger and watched the tall, slim figure of her fiancé overtake the two shorter, fatter friends. Tipping her straw sun hat over her eyes, Rose smiled in a detached way, watching the splashing from the sea, as if she were not really a part of the scene. As she closed her eyes, thoughts of her daughter's affairs came back to trouble her. Would life ever be the same again?

Dozing in a reverie, Rose suddenly realised the sun was being blocked out. As she opened her eyes, she saw a girl was standing in front of her.

'Hi, Mrs Collins, I thought that was you,' came a breathy little voice.

'Oh, Terrie, I didn't expect to see you here,' said Rose, removing her sunglasses.

'A day owing to me,' replied Terrie, arranging herself decoratively on the sand at Rose's feet. The white two-piece swimsuit she was wearing brought out her tan and her curves. Brunette curls peeped from beneath a turquoise spotted bandanna.

Rose shifted her weight on to her elbows. 'How is the office getting along without Amie?'

'We are managing, but we miss her, of course,' said Terrie. 'Are you here with friends? I am with someone. That's my fiancé, Dennis, over there.'

Terrie pointed to a shy young man standing gauchely in the background. Rose waved to him and he grinned self-consciously.

'So you are engaged!' remarked Rose. 'When is the wedding?'

'I thought Amie would have told you,' commented Terrie. 'We have to save some money before we can get married.'

With one supple movement, Terrie jumped to her feet and walked away, arms entwined, with her young man.

'So long,' said Rose wearily, sinking on to her back.

Amie had not told her mother of Terrie's engagement. In fact she had been completely reticent recently.

George arrived back from his dip in the sea and began to towel himself down vigorously. 'Nothing like a healthy swim!' he said cheerfully.

Wanda came puffing back, with Fred well in the rear. 'Oh dear, this calls for a cocktail,' she said with feeling.

George extended out a hand to Rose as she stood up. They walked hand in hand to the water's edge. In companionable silence, they paddled in the warm waves surging gently on to the smooth shore. Gradually, they entered deeper water and were suddenly lifted from their feet by the buoyant waves.

A swim helped to invigorate Rose and she emerged from the water feeling more lively. Digging her toes into the wet sand, she left a strange set of footprints. Laughter filled the air as she threw driftwood into the sea. George took a stick and engraved their entwined initials in the firm sand: GL/RC.

As they walked back to the loungers, George asked who the girl was who had been speaking to Rose.

'That was Terrie, Amie's secretary,' replied Rose.

'Pretty girl,' said George.

Rose towelled herself dry on her arrival back at the loungers. George looked elegant, even in his green and white swimming shorts she thought, looking at him admiringly. Wanda and Fred were already eating. Rose and George joined in enthusiastically, and drank toasts to each other with fruit juice. After eating their picnic lunch, they all lay in a row to digest their food. Each couple was surreptitiously holding hands, resting them on the warm sand, below the level of the loungers.

Towards evening they sat together, chatting, as the time drew near to leave. Fred announced out of the blue that he and Wanda were to marry. His fiancée giggled like a girl. George proclaimed this was a coincidence, as so were he and Rose.

This was the signal for mutual congratulations. They would have to celebrate the event. Not yet, but soon! The two women kissed each other and the two men shook hands.

Rose brought up the subject of Amie.

'I want to take her to Europe for a rest. Have any of you any suggestions as to where to go and how to finance the trip?'

George did not like the idea of discussing finances in front of the other two. 'We can discuss this later,' he insisted.

'Hold on a minute,' said Fred. 'We can work this out. I have some connections in England. You can stay there. If you can raise the fare we can come to some arrangement.'

'Sure, honey', said Wanda, 'we can help you.'

Rose wondered whether Amie's ex, Derek, could provide some of the money; about time he did something for her. George said he would help out but did not like the idea of being parted from his fiancée for long. There had certainly been a rash of engagements.

There was some hope now to lighten Rose's horizon. With the help of her friends, something could be done to provide Amie with future rest and hope of recovery. The two couples readied themselves for the journey home. The day on the beach had produced results for the worried woman.

Chapter Twenty-One

Amie had remained in hospital while she recovered from her nervous breakdown. To her the stay was timeless. Dreams and realities were merged in a never-ending stream of consciousness. Memories and desires darted teasingly in the dark corridors of her mind.

Coming out from this experience into a scenario of white uniforms and hot snacks, Amie began to relate to the real world. Familiar faces drew a response from her. Smiles became words as she began to interact with the nursing staff. Close family members were allowed to visit her.

When Rose brought her daughter home to convalesce, she found her a subdued shadow of her former self. Amie was put straight to bed and a regime of healthy feeding and gentle exercise began. A little light reading filled her waking hours. There were get well cards from various friends to show she was not alone.

Among her correspondence were two picture postcards depicting picturesque rural scenes from Robert James in England. He did not know of her prolonged illness and assumed her to be recovered from her injuries. The reason for his writing, so he said, was to see how she was getting on and to tell her of his circumstances. As he had connections, he was back working at his old place, living in London and spending weekends in the countryside.

Amie thought, Why should he write to me? But she put the cards away in her writing desk all the same. Poppy helped her mother to regain her health by sitting with her in the evenings and telling of her escapades at school. One day she asked when was Grandma taking her away for a vacation. What did this mean?

Amie got out of bed and went downstairs. 'Mom, what is this about a vacation?'

Rose looked up from her baking. 'Well, I'm glad to see you up and about. You must feel stronger. Sit at the table and I'll make you some coffee. Some of us have put together to pay for a trip to Europe for you.'

Amie sat at the kitchen table. Rose poured her a cup of fresh coffee, which her daughter sipped appreciatively. Strength was slowly flowing back into her limbs. Poppy came downstairs and sat at the table opposite her mother.

Poppy sat with her hair tied back with a ribbon and wearing a peppermint pink top and blue jeans. 'I'm staying with Daddy and Myrna while you are away.'

'Looks like everything has been arranged,' commented Amie, running her fingers through her hair.

'The change will do you good,' declared Rose.

'Everything sounds so wonderful. Who is paying for all this?' Amie asked.

'There's Derek, George, Fred and me. We are all helping in various ways,' Rose explained.

'England would be lovely. Spring should be there now,' mused Amie.

Rose and Poppy looked at each other and smiled knowingly. Amie stood up and looked in the kitchen mirror. There were bags under her eyes. The reflection of her pale face gazed wanly back at her.

'Mom, I look terrible,' complained Amie. 'Look at my hair! Why am I so thin? I have nothing to wear.'

Rose and Poppy laughed in relief. The little girl ran to her grandmother and hugged her.

'That's my girl!' exclaimed Rose. 'Welcome back.'

'Why did you say England, Mommy?' asked Poppy.

'I don't know, dear,' replied Amie. 'I must always have wanted to go there.'

That evening, Amie wrote a few lines to Robert James, via a box number in London, England, thanking him for his cards and explaining that she had been ill. Now that she was better, a trip to Europe was being planned for her and Rose.

The fact that Amie was showing interest in her appearance was a good sign. Rose encouraged this trait and made sure that plenty of rest and nourishing food built up her daughter's strength. This was to be a trip for her to relax and regain her confidence. Poppy was going to stay with her father while the two women were away on vacation, which pleased the child.

The trip was planned for the next month. Rose made sure that Amie built up her strength for the journey. There was also all the excitement of buying new clothes and packing. Betty Steiner visited to wish her friend good luck and a pleasant voyage.

Rose excused herself one evening, saying she had a previous engagement with her friends. The real reason was the celebration planned with George, Wanda and Fred for the double engagement celebration party. Amie was not informed of the plans in case she was upset by such an announcement. As yet she had to be kept quiet.

The party was held in a private room in an hotel. There was much jollity between the friends and facetious jokes were bandied about.

Towards the end of the festivities, Rose took George's hand and whispered in his ear. 'This has been a wonderful evening. Something to remember while we are parted. You are so good to me. I haven't laughed like this for weeks.'

George squeezed Rose's hand and drew her close to him. 'My darling, while you are away I don't know how I shall exist. All I want is your warmth near to me. You must phone me every day. I need you to come back soon to marry me.'

A combination of happiness and sadness caused tears to spring to Rose's eyes. George opened a bottle of champagne and poured out the sparkling stream. The company raised glasses in a silent toast. There was a pause while thoughts of the past and present went unspoken.

'We must do this next year on the same date,' gushed Wanda, breaking the silence.

'What a shame you two can't get married and take this trip as a honeymoon,' wheezed Fred, leaning back and undoing his waistcoat buttons to relieve his ample waist-line.

'You know this trip is for Amie and she must not have any pressure,' interposed George hastily, noticing the brightness in Rose's eyes.

'Never mind. Absence makes the heart grow fonder and we have all that to look forward to,' enthused Rose with forced gaiety, dabbing at her eyes with a tissue.

George stood up and raised his glass. 'I must say you two ladies look ravishing tonight, and I drink to your health.'

The two women preened as Rose glanced down at her white frilly blouse and black skirt. Wanda beamed delight-edly and smoothed down the skirt of her navy blue and white polka dotted two-piece suit.

Fred looked at the plates, containing the remnants of their meal, scattered on the snowy linen cloth. 'Shall we go on somewhere else?' he queried. 'Although I am not much of a dancer, I shall do so for the sake of my beloved.'

Wanda squealed with laughter as she sipped from her champagne glass. 'Oh yes, let's go on to a club,' she cried.

Rose agreed with this. 'I can't stay out too late. Amie might need me.'

The group left the restaurant and they all piled into a cab. Rose and Wanda soon found themselves side by side in the powder room of the Black Cat nightclub, repairing their make-up in front of a wall-length mirror. George and Fred waited for them at the bar. The place was crowded and filled with the chatter of myriad voices.

Rose gazed thoughtfully at herself in the mirror as she powdered her nose. 'I wonder whether I shall ever marry George,' she mused to herself.

Wanda vigorously applied lipstick to her cupid's bow, with appreciative glances at her appearance. 'Of course you shall, honey. Fred and I are tying the knot as soon as possible. Get that daughter of yours on her feet again and there'll be no holding you,' she affirmed, turning her head this way and that to get a back view of herself.

Chapter Twenty-Two

'Come along, let's dance,' suggested Rose, and led the way to the dance floor.

George joined his fiancée at the edge of the dance floor, took her in his arms and swept her smoothly into the throng. Rose rested her head on his shoulder, which was just the right height for her. They moved slowly round the dance floor as he held her close and breathed in the perfume of her hair. Fred and Wanda could be seen in the distance, performing their more energetic interpretation of the music.

'We are leaving soon, and I shan't see you for months,' murmured Rose.

'Will you miss me?' asked George.

'Not at all, you fool,' replied Rose, laughing. 'Seriously, though, I think that children can't imagine their parents having a love life.'

'You're right,' agreed George. 'They think we exist merely to act as babysitters and be useful to them. That is so in your case and some others I know. Luckily mine have moved away and I rarely see them.'

'You act as if you don't care,' protested Rose.

'Of course I care, but as long as they're all right and visit me at intervals that is fine with me,' said George.

'George, I want to spend the night with you,' Rose whispered in his ear. 'Something to remember while I am away.'

'Rose, darling, that is the best news I have had for many a day,' George enthused. 'There is plenty of life left in this old dog!'

He kissed her forehead as they danced, drawing her ever closer to him. Fred whisked by with Wanda, nodding at their friends as they whirled past. George laughed and Rose waved her hand at them. If only the night would last for ever!

At last even Wanda and Fred had enough nightclubbing. George and Rose dropped the other two off and took their cab to his apartment. The elevator purred smoothly upward to his floor, giving them the opportunity to kiss tenderly in the privacy of the moving container. The silver-haired man opened his apartment door with his key and ushered his fiancée into the living room.

'I love this room,' sighed Rose, kicking off her shoes and throwing her jacket on to the sofa.

'I have another room you'll love even more,' promised George.

They giggled like teenagers as George led Rose into the bedroom. The furnishings were comfortable but functional. Wine-coloured curtains and pale blue carpets made a pleasant contrast. The double bed beckoned enticingly.

George lifted Rose up in his arms and carried her over to his bed. 'We won't wait until the wedding,' he chortled.

Rose wriggled in his arms. 'You forget we've already done this,' she laughed.

'Never mind. This is another rehearsal,' George said, panting as he laid down his burden on the bed.

'Don't wear yourself out,' Rose warned, pulling herself up to rest her head on the pillow.

Without speaking, George removed his shoes and lay down next to her. Rose turned her face to his, accepting his kisses eagerly. With loving fingers, her fiancé undid her blouse and gently removed the garment from her. He caressed her body tenderly.

'You have such a beautiful figure, just like a young girl,' George whispered smoothly in her ear. He undid her skirt and slipped it down her legs.

'I think you are wonderful. The man of my dreams,' Rose replied. In her turn she undid his shirt, pulled him down to her and slid her arms round him beneath the white poplin material.

George pulled back the bed covers, and Rose slipped between the silk sheets. Shrugging off his clothes, the man joined her in the bed, wrapping her close in his arms.

Rose awoke early the next morning and gently shook George. 'I have to get back home,' she told him.

George held Rose tightly. 'Stay with me for a while,' he ordered, kissing her firmly and gently pulling her into his embrace.

At last Rose took her leave of George, promising to keep in touch. There was much to do at home to get ready for the trip. Poppy waylaid her grandmother as she hurried into the house, demanding to know where she had been. Amie's pale face peered over the banisters.

'I told you I was going out with some friends. Wanda put me up for the night,' explained Rose, feeling like a daughter having to explain herself to her parents.

'I wondered where you were!' complained Poppy.

'Come along, your father is going to pick you up. Let's get you ready,' Rose urged.

Hurrying up the stairs, Rose entered her bedroom and changed into casual clothes. Poppy's cases were almost packed. There were only a few things to add. The child's room was a mess, with things all over the place.

Amie came in to help. 'You don't mind coming on this trip with me, do you?' she asked her mother. 'I must be an awful burden to you.'

Rose assumed a cheerful manner. 'I am looking forward to the trip,' she assured her daughter. 'As soon as you get stronger, you are going to enjoy yourself and be your old self again.'

'Mom, I know you have a boyfriend. Is this serious for you?' Amie asked.

'Well, I do have someone. There is nothing that can't wait,' Rose replied, putting on a cheerful manner.

Derek Blake arrived to collect Poppy, who was driven away, rather excited at the change in her lifestyle. Amie and Rose watched the car disappearing into the distance and smiled at each other ruefully. They re-entered the house together. There was work to be done to finish the packing for their journey.

A week later, after flying to the East Coast for their connection, the two women were ensconced in a cabin on a cruise liner, ready for the crossing. There were flowers from friends and relatives to brighten the surroundings. An air of excitement filled the ship, as is usual on such occasions. After depositing their luggage, Amie and Rose took a stroll on deck to wave goodbye to the crowds, seeing off their friends and relatives.

'This is really exciting,' said Amie, waving her scarf at the retreating scene.

'Quite right,' agreed Rose, pleased to note some colour creeping into her daughter's cheeks.

As they turned to go down to the lower deck, Amie stumbled and was saved from falling by a strong arm which steadied her until she could stand upright again. Rose was shocked by her daughter's near accident. As she looked round a man took her elbow solicitously. The two women were drawn aside out of the crowd.

'Are you all right, madam?' asked a deep voice with an English accent. The man wore a uniform and was looking down at Amie.

'Oh yes, I seemed to trip,' replied Amie. The man was tall, dark and broad shouldered.

'You'll soon get your sea legs,' he replied, his brown eyes twinkling merrily. 'I am Rupert Fenwick, ship's doctor. If you have any trouble, come to see me.'

'Well, surely I shall,' Amie smiled.

Rupert Fenwick strode away, the breeze ruffling his thick black hair. Rose thought he looked nice. They might get acquainted. Perhaps he was the man to take Amie's mind off John Peters.

Chapter Twenty-Three

Rose and Amie made their way to their cabin to unpack. Their trunk and cases were already awaiting them. They had two single beds and a sea view. Sky and waves merged gently as the blurred line of the distant horizon moved gently up and down on the porthole.

'Let's just unpack our small bags and leave the trunks until later,' suggested Rose.

'Anything you say is fine,' agreed Amie. 'These clothes are all right for dinner.'

Rose saw from their schedule that dinner was a half-hour away. Quickly the two women unpacked their hand luggage and refreshed their make-up ready for dinner. They made their way up to the restaurant. The full-length mirrors situated at intervals along the corridors reflected their images flatteringly back at them.

Both women wore lightweight suits, Amie's being powder blue and straight skirted, whilst Rose's was light cream with a pleated skirt. As they approached the door of the restaurant, they were approached by a formidable-looking head waiter, who asked their names. They were identified on his list and admitted to the large bustling room. He ushered them to a table in the centre of the restaurant.

'That head waiter acted like we were stowaways,' complained Amie. 'Perhaps they don't like women alone.'

'We're not alone,' soothed Rose. 'We are together, dear.'

There was a middle-aged couple at their table, who introduced themselves as Bob and Ida Turner. In no time at all, they had recited their life stories and their reason for the crossing: to visit married children. The couple seemed pleasant enough, but Rose did not want to disclose too much about her and Amie's business. Anything they said would probably do the rounds of the ship before tomorrow.

'We thought we might get on the Captain's table,' complained Bob, frowning and adjusting his horn-rimmed glasses.

'My husband is very big in industry,' interposed Ida, nodding in agreement.

'I wonder whether that nice Doctor Fenwick is going to be on our table,' muttered Rose in Amie's ear.

'What is that dear?' demanded Ida leaning forward and cupping her ear.

'My mother said the decor is lovely in here,' responded Amie, waving her hand to indicate the red plush furnishings and twinkling chandeliers.

'Not bad,' said Bob. 'We have been in finer ships but this one is about average.'

Another couple were ushered to their table; a big fat husband and a little thin wife. Ida and the thin woman clicked immediately and were soon chattering away together like old friends. Bob and the fat man started boasting to each other of their business exploits. The meal commenced with the table hosted, not by the handsome Rupert Fenwick, but by another plainer and more taciturn officer.

Ida, resplendent in flashy jewels and red cabbage rose patterned gown, tried to monopolise the conversation with the officer, who proved to be Kenneth Appleby, the gym instructor.

Amie became rather bored during dinner, and drew lines on the white tablecloth with her fork. Now what did that remind her of? There had been a canary coloured checked tablecloth and someone in a rough tweed jacket. Becoming thoughtful, she remembered serious grey eyes in a concerned face as someone tried to warn her of danger.

'Amie!' The sharp tone of her mother's voice brought her abruptly back to the present. Dinner was over and everyone was adjourning to the various bars and dance floors.

The two women rose from the table and walked to the deck. As they strolled along the breezy walkway, Rose remarked that Amie had seemed distant.

'I was remembering things, from a great distance,' replied Amie. 'Some events seem vague. Gradually everything is beginning to fall into place. My life is one big jigsaw.'

Rose did not understand all of this but surely trying to rationalise events was a good sign. Amie shivered and suggested leaving the chill Atlantic breeze. They bade farewell to the dark of the night with the pale etched moon and went into the nearest bar for two dry martinis. Feeling warmer, they both began to cheer up.

As they left the bar to find the ballroom, a deep voice called to them. Strong hands grasped the two women by their elbows. Rose looked up enquiringly. Rupert Fenwick was looking down at her with velvety brown eyes.

'I remember you two beautiful ladies from this afternoon,' he said. 'Are you enjoying yourselves or can I help?'

'We are just going to dance,' replied Rose.

'Allow me to accompany you,' said Rupert, offering an arm to each one. 'We have to make sure the passengers have a happy voyage.'

As Rupert accompanied the two women to the ballroom, he explained that not all his duties were pleasant. Not all the passengers were as agreeable as they were. Some were always complaining about something or other. He complimented the ladies on their beauty and asked whether they were sisters.

'I am Rose Collins, and this is my daughter, Amie Blake,' said Rose, laughing politely.

'My mother always looks young and I look old because I have been ill,' added Amie with a wry smile.

Rupert guided them into the ballroom. 'I am sorry you have been ill. Is this a trip to recuperate?'

Amie looked up at him with her clear green eyes. 'Yes, Rupert, this vacation is a present from my mother and some dear friends.'

Rupert danced first with Rose. He held her firmly, his hand on her back as he guided her expertly around the floor.

'You are a wonderful dancer, Rose,' he complimented her.

'One of my hobbies,' Rose explained. 'I think dancing is so relaxing.'

'Same here, so do I,' agreed Rupert.

'Amie has found a partner,' remarked Rose, as her daughter swept by in the arms of Kenneth Appleby. 'He is the officer on our table.'

'I want to dance with your daughter,' said Rupert. 'What lovely eyes she has! I almost regret I am married.'

Rose felt disappointed at those words. Amie must not get mixed up with another man who was not free. Rupert guided his partner across the floor. He called out to Kenneth and the two men changed partners as the music ended.

As the music began again, Amie found herself dancing in Rupert's arms. They moved rhythmically in time to the beat. This pastime was undemanding for her and she could let the room flow around her. Reveries and dreams filled her head.

'Are you all right?' Rupert's voice invaded her head.

Amie jumped, then laughed. 'I was relaxing too much,' she explained.

'Would you like to talk?' asked Rupert.

'Why don't you tell me about yourself?' replied Amie.

Rupert told of his wife and children at home. He was going to leave the cruise ship after the next trip for a job nearer home. Susan, his wife, was not happy during his long absences. He squeezed Amie gently but there was no response.

'I was telling your mother you have lovely eyes,' Rupert remarked. 'They are so sad, though.'

Amie looked solemnly up at him.

Chapter Twenty-Four

The rest of the crossing passed in much the same manner. Amie was pursued by the married Rupert Fenwick. As is widely known, there is a custom of not dressing for dinner on the first night at sea. Therefore, although the suit she wore on the first evening flattered her, she looked even lovelier wearing evening dress on the subsequent nights.

Rose looked striking too, and the two ladies drew appreciative glances from the men aboard the ship. Rupert's obvious attention to Amie annoyed the young woman's mother. Although she had thought he might be a suitable companion for her daughter, the fact that he was married and his conspicuously flirtatious manner, earned her disapproval. However, apart from this, the time passed pleasantly enough.

Amie was polite to Rupert and was pleased to drink and dance with him, while keeping him at arm's length. One evening however, he caught her off guard. A barbecue was announced on deck in the open air. Rose did not want to attend and stayed below to play cards with some new friends.

Amie and Rupert ascended to the top deck and stepped through the doorway onto the dimly-lit boards. They walked forward together into the darkness. The barbecue was being held round the corner of the deckhouse. The smell of cooking wafted on the night air and the sound of voices drifted in from the party.

There were rows of chairs in a little shelter to the left. Rupert guided Amie inside, where they could stand out of the breeze. He pressed her against the wall. His silhouette was clearly visible to her in the darkness against the washed-out hues of the night sky.

Amie felt Rupert's lips brush softly against hers. His hands touched her hair and traced the outline of her face. More urgently, his mouth moved against hers. Firmly holding her waist with one hand, he caressed her neck and shoulders with the other.

Nothing was said during these few moments. The sound of their breathing was the only noise to break the silence. Rupert's breathing was becoming harsh and quick. Amie was surprised to find herself responding to his ardour.

The feel of a man's body pressed urgently against hers, triggered off the responses she thought had gone for ever. Amie was wearing an off the shoulder long white evening gown, and the touch of Rupert's hands wandering over her bare flesh made her tingle with desire. He was a tall, broad man, just right for a woman to put her arms round and hug tightly. Without making any conscious decision, she was kissing him back fiercely, holding his face in her two hands and feeling the stubble on his chin beneath her fingers.

Rupert pulled Amie away from the wall and fumbled with the back of her gown. His trembling fingers undid the fastenings and he pulled down the bodice. He bent his head to kiss her neck. The touch of his caressing hands on her breasts was tantalising, for both of them.

Rupert undid his uniform jacket to bring Amie inside against his chest. 'Should I apologise, my little girl?' he whispered huskily. 'I didn't plan this but you are so lovely. Say the word and I shall stop, although I really don't want to. You seem to want the same thing so I hope we can go on, or I shall explode!'

Amie put her arms round his waist inside his jacket and kissed his cheek. 'I was expecting you to make a pass,' she murmured softly. 'What I wasn't expecting was my feelings. You have taken me by surprise. My heart is going boom-te-boom and I'm floating on pink clouds.'

Rupert's response was a murmur of pleasure as he brushed his face against the smoothness of her hair. He sat Amie on a chair and knelt before her to hug and caress her. There were some blankets on the deck chairs in the corner. Taking these, he made a bed on the floor by the illumination from his lighter.

Amie was shivering by then. The heat of Rupert's body, as he enveloped her in his arms, soon cured her trembling as they made reckless love to each other. His warmth possessed her like an encompassing eiderdown. As they lay on the blankets, at the end of a long kiss, their passion was sated.

Gasping and wiping his forehead, Rupert sat up and leaned on his elbows. Amie lay there exhausted. He bent down to kiss her nose. Trying to straighten her clothes, she got to her feet.

'Let me help you,' said Rupert, beginning to fasten the back of the gown for her. 'Well, you can't say we Englishmen are terrible lovers.'

'Englishmen!' said Amie, as if she were reminded of something she had momentarily forgotten. 'You were great, but I am mixed up and angry with myself.'

'Is something wrong, my sweet?' asked Rupert. 'You seem to have suddenly changed.'

'No, when you said "Englishmen" – never mind,' replied Amie. 'We should not have done this, that's what is wrong. I forgot about everything. Your marriage; a shipboard romance.'

In fact, Amie made the latter statement to hide her thoughts about another Englishman. Why she should feel guilty, yes guilty, about making love with a ship's officer, when another Englishman she hardly knew seemed to hover like a disapproving uncle above her, was beyond her understanding. Could she do nothing without feeling that sanctimonious, solicitous gaze on her? The thought of Robert James had come unbidden into the mind of the young woman, standing in the dark with another man, as soon as the word 'Englishmen' was mentioned.

Amie made excuses not to go to the barbecue and hurried to her cabin, leaving the bewildered ship's doctor standing in the shadows of the deck. He scratched his head and gazed after her retreating figure. He could hear the sound of passengers laughing and the rhythmic beat of music in the distance. The intermittent splashing of waves as the bow cut through the mighty volume of water came faintly through the darkness.

In her cabin, Amie threw herself onto her bed and wept. What a fool she was! Some madness had made her behave that way with a man she hardly knew. Rupert must think she was one of those tramps of the ocean.

Amie jumped up impulsively from the bed and looked at herself in the mirror. A bedraggled wide-eyed hag stared back at her. Her long white evening gown was creased, ripped and reminded her of that evening's activities. With frenzied movements, she tore the offending garment from her body and stuffed it and her underwear into the waste bin.

Pausing only to put a shower cap over her hair, Amie stepped into the shower and began to cleanse herself in the purifying water. The streams ran down her face and body, as she tried to lose herself in the washing routine. When she became tired of this, she put on a light blue robe and sat before the mirror to cream her face. Next she washed her hair and wrapped a towel round her head.

When Rose arrived back at the cabin, which was in darkness, she switched on the light and found her daughter fast asleep in bed. Around her head on the pillow were spread damp tendrils of hair. Beneath the coverlet, the pink glow on her cheeks and the fans of her eyelashes made her look angelic, innocent even!

Rose saw the torn clothes in the waste bin and the damp towels thrown on the floor of the bathroom. Oh no! Surely Amie had not got herself entangled with that married officer. Hoping that life was not about to become even more complicated, the older woman followed the routine of removing her make-up and then undressed, ready to go to bed.

Lying in the darkness, listening to the regular breathing of her daughter, Rose thought of her George and wondered whether he thought of her. His sapphire engagement ring was on her finger and she twisted the hard circle round in an absent-minded manner as she tried to sleep. At last dreams of happier times came to her. Then the alarm clock woke her abruptly.

Rose looked over at Amie, who was lying there asleep in the same position as last night. 'Get up, nearly time for breakfast,' she called, getting out of bed.

Amie yawned and stretched. 'I'm awake, don't worry,' she replied, then a look of unhappiness came into her eyes as she remembered the events of the previous night.

Chapter Twenty-Five

There were only a few days remaining before the ship docked in England. Amie avoided Rupert, who hovered hopefully in her environs. His pleading glances and attempts at reconciliation met with a cold refusal to discuss the events of that evening. The young woman definitely wanted to forget the whole thing.

Rose did not discuss the matter with Amie. Perhaps the trip had been a bad idea. Bringing her on the ship to meet suitable men had not worked out. Something had happened that had built a wall between mother and daughter.

Therefore the end of the crossing brought relief to several of the passengers. The two couples at their restaurant table were becoming even more irritating to Rose and, to a certain extent, to Amie. Ida Turner and the thin woman, Enid Lambert, chattered and gossiped incessantly. Bob Turner and the thin woman's husband, Victor Lambert, never ceased to talk about business and getting the better of the other fellow.

Ida's brightly-coloured clothes and shrewd piggy little eyes grated on Rose's usually calm nature. Enid's awful old-fashioned fashion sense – a maroon frock with pleated drapes arranged across her flat chest and artificial flowers pinned on one shoulder – was especially annoying. Their smug self-assurance that their values were right and anyone disagreeing with them was wrong, and their insinuating, disparaging remarks about all and sundry, made them bad representatives of their country. They tutted and disapproved continuously.

Bob, with his shiny bald head and expansive waistcoat decorated with an obtrusive watch-chain, was nothing but a loud snob. Victor, enormously fat and wheezy, was secretly lecherous; ever darting sly glances at passing girls. The officer at their table, Kenneth Appleby, was not much of a conversationalist. Although he had danced several times with both Rose and Amie, he seemed to think he had done his duty and need not pretend to be friendly.

Together with this, and the fact that Rupert Fenwick was someone who needed to be avoided, the crossing would not seem to have been a complete success. The women were glad that the end was in sight. Neither of them had mentioned *that* night. They thought any discussion might cause an argument.

At the last night dance, Amie could not avoid dancing with Rupert. There was the risk of causing a scene by a refusal to speak.

He danced her round the floor, asking 'Why are you giving me the cold shoulder?'

'That seems pretty obvious,' she replied, 'In the circumstances your attentions are embarrassing and I wish you would get the heck away from me.'

'I thought we had something special,' Rupert confided.

'I expect you say that to some woman on every trip,' Amie retorted.

'Be fair!' was the indignant reply. 'You didn't exactly fight me.'

'No, you are right,' came the subdued rejoinder, surprising him. 'I think I am more mad with myself than anything else.'

'Let's have a drink and part good friends,' suggested Rupert, hoping to regain her affection. 'I thought you were wonderful the other night.'

'I don't think so,' said Amie emphatically, looking up at those deep brown eyes and wavy black hair. One look at his face and she would be lost again. To dive into the dark comforting cradle of his embrace would be lovely... but this action would be unwise and she knew must be avoided as an addictive drug. 'Not this time, Rupert, but thanks for the offer,' she said firmly.

Rupert shrugged with good-natured surrender. He was hurt, but there would be other girls. There were not many as lovely and passionate as this one. What a shame his wife had insisted on his leaving the ship.

As the dance came to an end, Rupert bent down and kissed Amie on the lips gently. 'Come outside for a moment,' he entreated. 'Honestly, no funny business.'

Amie looked at him and nodded. 'All right, just for a minute,' she agreed. 'I shall trust you.'

They went out on to the deck, and he drew her slowly towards him. They began to dance again in the dark, slowly, to the music. 'There you are now,' Rupert soothed her quietly. 'I know you think I have a reputation. With you I feel special. There is a magic that draws me to you.'

Snuggling up against him, Amie sighed. 'I have just got out of one relationship where the man was already involved with someone else. That led to a car accident. Also I had a nervous breakdown. Now I can't face anything like that again, although I love feeling your arms so close around me; I want to stay like this forever, and you are about the most handsome man I have ever seen.'

Rupert led the way to a dark corner by the rails. He took Amie in his arms and kissed her thoroughly. 'Didn't the fact ever occur to you that I might feel exactly the same about you? I feel like a helpless fool.'

Amie raised her flushed face to his and groaned. This was not meant to happen again with Rupert. 'Do you feel the same as I do? I am as weak as a kitten,' she said.

They looked into each other's faces in the gloom, then clung to each other. The night flowed round them and left them alone. To stand there forever, not moving, would be paradise. The sound of couples laughing and music playing floated on the cool air.

They found a dark corner among the sunbeds for their embraces. There was a strange desperation in their love-making. After a timeless eternal moment had passed, Amie slowly moved her face away from the cosy niche on Rupert's shoulder. They kissed each other tenderly in the shadows of the awning.

Rupert sighed, 'Yes, I know this is all wrong. I have a wife and two little boys. If we carry on I shall hurt you as well. You must not be upset again, I can see. But you are so irresistible, nothing else seems to matter.'

Amie pulled herself to her feet, making an effort to stifle a sob, 'I don't know why you had this effect on me or why I let this happen. We might run into each other again. You never know what's round the corner. In the meantime, Rupert, have a good life.'

As she walked away, Rupert's voice followed, urgently. 'We must keep in touch!' His footsteps rapidly gained on her and his hand touched her arm.

Amie was distraught and she cried out, 'We should have kept apart tonight; this has made parting worse!' Squeezing his hand for a moment, she turned and walked off to her cabin.

Rose was in there, putting a finishing touch to her packing. A sharp look at her daughter made her sigh.

'Oh, there you are, dear. Are you through with your packing? There's lots to look forward to. We'll see England tomorrow, for the first time.'

'All right, fine by me.' Amie smiled brightly and began gathering her belongings together. Soon the cabin began to look more tidy. All was ready for the morning. Cases and trunks were placed in a neat row convenient for disembarking.

'Now, dear, back to the party for a drink,' said Rose.

Amie went in the bathroom to fix her lipstick and comb her hair. The reflection that stared back at her looked haunted and miserable. Despite herself, she began to giggle. Love was supposed to make you happy – and look at her past record!

Rose and Amie went to the ballroom and had a drink. They danced with each other for the last waltz and wore paper hats. Streamers were suspended with informal abandon from the ceiling. The orchestra began to play 'Auld Lang Syne' and everyone retired for the night, some to their own cabins!

'Come on, tomorrow is another day,' said Amie, leading the way to their cabin. Rose followed on, hoping that tomorrow would be a happier day.

Chapter Twenty-Six

Let us draw a veil over the next morning. There was the usual hustle and bustle of a ship berthing and the passengers disembarking at Southampton. Stewards conveyed the heavy luggage to the deck and waited discreetly for their tips. Goodbyes were said and unreal promises to keep in touch with newly acquired friends were made.

There was no time to think of sadness or regrets. Rose and Amie breakfasted early and busied themselves in packing their night-clothes and toilet articles. They ascended to the deck. Before very long they found themselves ushered ashore to the tender mercies of England.

There was no sign of Rupert. That was only to be expected. Rose hoped they would never see him again and Amie could not hope to see him again. They nodded and waved to acquaintances made on the ship.

Ida and Enid, dressed in their smart suits, were still chattering away nineteen to the dozen. They nodded sagely at Rose and Amie, chirping brightly at them that they must meet up in England; in the meantime secretly exchanging dark secrets about other passengers' private lives. Bob and Victor slapped each other fraternally on the shoulders as they exchanged business cards. Both glanced appraisingly at Rose and Amie as the two women edged their way through the crowd to the gangway.

Someone was there to meet Rose and Amie: Henry Brown, a business connection of Fred Martin. He drove them to an hotel and gave them their first glimpse of England.

Rose was alarmed. 'You're driving on the wrong side of the road!' she exclaimed, and immediately laughed, realising her mistake.

Henry Brown chortled, his chins beneath his bald head quivering. 'I can tell you haven't been here before,' he retorted in a mock patronising manner.

Amie thought the houses and shops were small and quaint. They settled in an hotel for a few days. A house would soon be made available for them. Henry was in real estate like Fred Martin.

'So this is Southampton,' commented Amie, peering through the dingy lace curtains of the narrow window in their bedroom.

'This is not so bad,' comforted Rose.

Henry had secured a house in Sussex for them. He said they would be nearer to London, where they could visit the shops and the theatres. Rose and Amie were looking forward to that. Meanwhile, they would acclimatise themselves on England's south coast.

Amie complained of the cold. Rose fiddled about, trying to get some heat from the radiator. The weather was heavy and bleak. Perhaps they turned the heat off for the summer, however dismal the season turned out to be.

'I hope this is not normal English weather,' complained Amie. 'I wish we had gone somewhere warmer.'

'You know you wanted to come to England,' Rose pointed out. 'Let's go out for a walk and cheer ourselves up.'

So mother and daughter put on their warm coats and, linking arms, set out to explore Southampton. They went into an English pub for their lunch. There were objects with a nautical theme, attached to the walls and hanging from the ceiling, such as ropes and an anchor. When the landlord heard their accent, he engaged them in conversation.

The other drinkers joined in the conversation, keen to learn about LA. By the time Rose and Amie left the pub at closing time, they were flushed and laughing; their opinion of England was hastily revised. The natives were definitely friendly, and not least, they had been promised by all the experts in the pub that the good weather was just around the corner. If not, they could always come back to the pub for a drink.

Many of the shops in the High Road sold picture postcards. Rose paused in her perambulation to look at them and wondered aloud at the pictures of big fat ladies in tight red costumes and little thin men in blue-striped baggy outfits, paddling in the sea.

'This must be the English sense of humour,' said a puzzled Amie. 'Shall we send some cards home?'

'Oh yes,' agreed Rose. 'Poppy would love some.'

They selected a dozen cards each to friends and relatives. Back in their hotel room, there was silence for a while as they wrote messages on the backs. The cards they had chosen portrayed scenes of Southampton; not those vulgar comic ones. Rose sent one to George, saying how much she missed him.

'Would you like some tea?' Amie asked. 'Or shall we wait for dinner?'

'We can make our own,' replied Rose, indicating the little table set with cups and tea bags.

'At least they have that,' commented Amie.

'Shall I be mother?' asked Rose, attempting to bring some levity into the conversation.

Rose and Amie drank their tea and took turns to bath and get ready for dinner. The dining room was in a depressing downstairs back room with lace curtained windows and claustrophobically close tables. Strangely enough, they both felt exposed, being placed in the middle of the room. Every head was raised when they entered the room and every pair of eyes seemed to bore through their backs, as the silent eating and drinking went on.

A sullen looking middle-aged woman in a black and white uniform took their order. A wait of ten minutes produced the soup. Twenty minutes later came the main dish. As soon as was decently possible, the two women left the dining room.

'I can't possibly stay in this place,' complained Rose to Henry, phoning from their hotel bedroom. 'The food is awful, the service grudging, we are cold and Amie is depressed.'

'I am so sorry,' apologised Henry. 'That was only a temporary arrangement. This seems to be a peak time and there was not much room in the best hotels. Good news! I have the keys to your house and you can go there tomorrow.'

'Thank goodness for that,' rejoiced Rose. 'Amie and I are ready to go any time.'

Henry came to see them that evening and took them out to a welcoming bar. He made sympathetic noises as they sipped dry martinis and gradually relaxed in the atmosphere. A music tape played in the background. They sat at a table in a secluded corner.

'I feel I can relax here,' Amie admitted suddenly. 'That place was really winding me up.'

'I don't think they like Americans here,' agreed Rose. 'There was a hostile atmosphere.'

'That was probably because most of the clientele are long-stay customers and a stranger is a curiosity to them,' Henry said, excusing himself from any guilt in the matter. 'Anyway, I have the papers and the keys ready for you to go away tomorrow to a lovely village in Sussex. All instructions for the move are in this envelope. Fred said I have to take very special care of you.'

His eyes twinkled and he grinned at them boyishly. Rose smiled back politely. The rest of the evening passed uneventfully. Henry danced with each lady in turn, telling both how he missed LA and couldn't wait to get back there.

Next day, Rose and Amie hastened to get packed and leave the hotel. Henry promised to have their trunks sent on. At the station he kissed them both and shook hands. He waved after the departing train, then rushed off thankfully to other unfinished business waiting for him.

Rose leaned back in her seat. 'What a relief to get away,' she intoned. 'I hope this Sussex is better.'

Amie looked through the train window at the fields and telegraph poles rushing past. 'Look at all this green countryside. I am beginning to feel relaxed already.'

Chapter Twenty-Seven

Rose smiled benignly at her daughter. Perhaps when they were settled in their house things would get better. They needed peace and quiet. Amie had become wild and irrational in her thoughts and actions and must settle down in her mind for her own good.

The older woman read a paperback novel and Amie actually slept throughout most of that train journey. Neither of them had realised how tired the younger woman still was. That nightmare of the accident and the let-down by John Peters had left their mark. The unfortunate occurrence of the episode with Rupert Fenwick could be a setback in her recovery, as she was more vulnerable than she realised at the moment and could become attracted to anyone who paid her attention.

Rose instinctively knew that the sensitive young woman must heal her own body and mind. The confused and uncertain state she was in could cause her to throw herself into unwise affairs without thinking, as she had done with Rupert Fenwick on the ship. The train sped through the day, cutting a swathe through the lush green countryside. Best to relax and let events take their course as she, too, felt her eyes close for a little doze.

Before they arrived at their station, she had already awoken from her brief snooze. Feeling refreshed, she shook her daughter gently.

'Wake up,' she said quietly. 'We are here now.'

Amie stretched and yawned. What a lovely sleep that had been; so restful and refreshing.

'Oh fine,' she muttered. 'Where is here, then?'

Soon she regained her equilibrium and was ready to alight when the train arrived at the station. They were almost the only passengers to leave. A group of youths in school uniform got off and rushed noisily away. A tall man left from the next compartment.

Amie jumped nervously. For a moment she thought the man was Robert James but at second sight he was not at all like him. How stupid of her! He was hardly likely to be travelling on the same train as them on the same day.

Rose had not noticed the resemblance as she had not yet met Robert James. A quick glance from Amie at her mother, though, betrayed her confusion. What had happened now, and why was she staring at that other passenger? They must find a porter and leave this station as soon as possible.

Hastily she waved at a uniformed figure leaning nonchalantly against a luggage trolley.

'Hey, are you a porter?' she called.

The man turned his head slowly in the direction of her voice. 'Yes, that's right,' he agreed.

'Could you give us a hand here?' asked Amie.

The man shambled slowly towards them. 'Righty-ho,' he said.

In spite of his lack of speed, the porter produced a luggage trolley and soon had their cases neatly piled up. Rose asked for the stationmaster.

'I'm the stationmaster,' said the porter.

'Oh great,' said Rose, becoming confused. 'I need transport to this address, also my trunks are coming on behind and I need to be informed when they arrive.'

The stationmaster looked at the address on the paper that Rose showed him. He spat out the tobacco he was chewing, and spoke.

'Fair enough,' he agreed. 'We'll let you know, missus.'

A lanky youth appeared, who helped load the luggage on board a disreputable-looking black taxi. The driver appeared from the little café situated conveniently adjacent to the station.

'Get in, love,' he said. 'I'll soon get you there, special rates.'

Rose and Amie manoeuvred themselves into the back of the taxi, which lurched into action and hurtled off down the country lane leading from the station. The driver, who had tousled brown hair and a pencil sticking out from behind his ear, turned his head companionably as he drove, to speak to his passengers.

'You were lucky there, love,' he remarked. 'I just finished me tea break.'

Rose said, 'Really, are you the only driver?' hoping he would turn his head to the front and thus avoid some terrible collision with oncoming traffic.

The driver scratched his head and continued turning his head to the back at regular intervals.

'You American, are you?' he asked. 'Don't worry, I never had a crash yet; I know these roads like the back of me hands,' he averred, demonstrating the fact by removing his hands from the wheel and displaying the backs of them to his passengers.

Rose began to wonder whether he was sane. Amie gazed fixedly through the taxi window, her complexion pale and her mouth set in a straight line. A snort of laughter came from the front seat and made the two women jump. The driver looked round again and winked roguishly.

'Just me little joke,' he explained. 'I'm a Londoner; had to come out to the fresh air for my health, for asthma you know. My family comes from round here, so I come back to live.'

After a while Rose began to relax as the taxi hurtled along the winding lanes. Amie leaned back and closed her eyes.

'Soon be there, now,' commented the driver, facing the front for a change. 'Nice little house; you staying there long?'

'Just for the summer,' replied Rose.

'Nice little spot, quiet and peaceful,' ruminated the driver. 'The sun's coming out too, you mark my words.'

So saying, he swung the taxi round a sharp corner and screeched to a sudden halt in a leaf shaded cul-de-sac. Rose and Amie sat motionless for a while, thankful to be safe.

The driver leapt from the cab and threw open the door. 'Here you are, ladies, Beech View. If you want me, the name's Ernie. You'll get me at the station. Good luck and goodbye.'

He pocketed the five pound note which Rose proffered, eased his crumpled grey suited form into the cab and drove rapidly away, waving his hand as he went. Amie turned towards the house. Walking towards the gate, she looked along the flower-bordered garden path. A high privet hedge surrounded the whole site, giving privacy and shade.

Lined up meticulously outside the perimeter of the garden, giant trees brushed the tops of the hedges with their leaf-burdened branches, swinging clusters of tiny white blossoms to and fro in the breeze. Amie gazed at the house, which was waiting quietly and expectantly for them. The low roof frowned mildly, framing the wide windows of eyes. Centrally, in the front elevation of the house, stood the stout front door, waiting for the new guests to walk through to the comfort inside.

Rose liked the house. 'Come on, in we go,' she said.

Amie was drawn to the building before her. 'This house has been waiting for me,' she murmured.

Rose fumbled in her purse for the keys. Amie rested her hand gently on the smooth green-painted top bar of the gate. Snapdragons and pansies nodded like wide-eyed innocents in the flower beds. Pushing the gate open, she walked slowly along the crazy paving which formed the path and stood by the step, resting her hand flat against the light bronze varnish of the door.

Rose hurried along the path towards Amie and inserted the key into the lock. The door swung smoothly open on the well-oiled hinges and remained wide open for the women to enter. Inside was a sturdy coir doormat. Fitted carpets, patterned in russet and gold, awaited their tread on the downstairs floors and stairs.

'Very nice,' said Rose appreciatively.

'What a wonderful place, waiting here for me,' whispered Amie happily.

This was hers, to love and cherish. Living here was all she wanted, that is for the moment.

Chapter Twenty-Eight

Rose put her cases down on the hall carpet just inside the front door. Amie hurried inside and began her eager tour of the house. Not for a long while had she been so interested in anything. Without a pause, she set out to explore all the rooms.

The house was neatly bisected by a long, narrow, red-tiled passage. From a position at the back of the house, facing the front door, an old fashioned lounge could be seen on the right. There was a comfortable suite, covered in a rural chintz fabric in this room. Matching full-length curtains concealed the french windows which led to the back garden.

In front of the fireplace lay a beige deep-pile rug. On the walls hung several strategically placed watercolours of landscapes and seascapes.

The modern kitchen was on the left of the passage. There were all the modern conveniences, including cooker, refrigerator, dishwasher, and washing machine. Above the sink was a blue and white curtained window, with a view of the back garden. The room was freshly painted in eau-de-Nil and the back door had thick glass panels in the top half.

There was a note on one of the work surfaces, to the effect that the back door key was on the keyring and explaining the position of the fuses. Amie decided to continue her tour of the house before looking at the garden.

To the right of the front door was a cupboard for coats and boots. Next to that there was a toilet and shower tucked away in a recess. The passage gave way to a little carpeted alcove. From there the quaint staircase, complete with dark-stained carved banisters, led to the first floor.

The living room was on the left of the front door. The bay window, looking onto the front garden, boasted pretty sprigged curtains with, peeping coyly between them, a frilled fine veil of lace falling from the pleated pelmet. A magnificent sideboard stood against one wall. Against the other wall was a highly-polished folding table and four sturdy cushioned chairs, so that the room could be used as a dining room.

Amie could hear Rose walking about upstairs, so she ran up the narrow staircase to join her. Neither of them had spoken since they had opened the front door. There would be plenty to say to each other later. Exploring a new place was always rather exciting.

Amie found Rose admiring the front bedroom. Matching wallpaper and curtains, patterned with deep crimson and pale pink roses, decorated the walls and windows. The casement window in the room nestled snugly in the eaves. There was an attractive view through the window at the front garden and the low-hanging boughs of the bordering trees.

'This must be your room,' she announced. 'Look at all the lovely roses to pay tribute to your name.'

'You haven't seen the other bedroom yet,' replied her mother with a little laugh. 'That one is smaller.'

Amie returned to the landing and ran up the two steps leading to the back bedroom. The ceiling sloped downwards from the side to accommodate the shape of the roof. There was therefore one short wall and one tall wall. A cushioned window seat chest lay before the narrow mullioned window and the bed rested against the high wall.

This smaller room was decorated with warm colours which Amie loved. The wallpaper pattern consisted of shades of cream and gold in abstract swirls, and the curtains were adorned with impressions of sunflowers. All the carpets upstairs were of a dark chestnut brown colour. The view from the window showed a tangle of flowers and bushes, all growing together in colourful profusion.

'Yes, this is my room,' she called out, turning to see her smiling mother framed in the doorway. 'Why, even the colour could have been picked for me.'

'I am so glad you are pleased with the house,' said Rose, putting her arm round her daughter's shoulder. 'I said we only wanted a small place, but comfortable.'

The two women looked in at the upstairs bathroom and toilet in the other slope of the roof. Birds were twittering outside and flying past the windows. There was an airing cupboard on the landing. A little trapdoor in the ceiling led to a tiny attic.

Amie flew down the stairs for the treat she had been saving until last. As she grasped the doorknob to the back door, she remembered that the key was on the ring.

'Mom, give me the keys,' she called up the stairs.

Rose emerged from her bedroom, where she had been snatching a few minutes' rest on the bed. Hurrying down the stairs, she picked up the keys from the hall table and took them into the kitchen.

'What is the matter now?' she complained, handing over the keys.

Amie examined the keys and tried them in the back door. A big old-fashioned key fitted the lock. The young woman turned the doorknob and the door swung easily open. Breathing in the fresh air, she stepped outside.

A crazy paving path led up one side of the garden. The lawn alongside was growing wildly and was well in need of a trim. Flowering creepers clung tenaciously to the fence on both sides. The part just in front of the house was paved and boasted a few over-sized flower pots.

On each side of the garden was a flower bed, planted out with a multiplicity of blooms. They were of all shapes and sizes and Amie did not know the names of most of them. Blossoming fruit trees could be seen to the rear of the flower beds. The whole garden was surrounded by an encompassing darkly creosoted wooden fence.

Amie continued walking along the path and came to a small shed, leaning against the left-hand fence. The door sagged open and she could see inside some garden chairs and a round table. Various garden tools and a lawnmower were strewn about or propped against the walls, ready for use by the gardener.

Further down the garden she came upon overgrown bushes and an archway, embraced and crowned by climbing pale mauve sweet peas and deep red roses, growing one each side. A rustic seat was set artistically on a small circular lawn between the arch and the bushes. This was a secret little place to hide with your thoughts. Nearby, hollyhocks and sunflowers raised their majestic heads above the common crowd.

Positioned at the far end of the garden were a clump of mature trees. One of them was an enormous beech tree. Massive boughs leaned down heavily towards the ground. The claw-like roots formed sinewy shapes on the earth.

Leaves formed a curtain in front of the tree. Ducking her head, Amie crept into the space previously hidden from her view. In there she came on an unexpected sight. Thick ropes were tied to a convenient thick bough and hung down like the plaits of a Nordic goddess.

A wooden seat formed the base of a swing. *How lovely!* Amie thought. *This must have been here for years*. The ropes squeaked gently as she sat tentatively on the seat and began swinging slowly to and fro.

Many questions wandered like unwelcome guests through Amie's mind. The gently creaking bough above her accepted her presence stoically, as she swung rhythmically, eyes closed in reverie. There was something about this place. After all, who would rent out a lovely house like this that seemed as if the owner had just stepped out for a minute and would soon be returning?

Amie heard a voice in the distance and gradually came back to the present. Rose was calling her name and sounded quite alarmed. The swing gradually came to a standstill. Footsteps were approaching softly across the grass.

Amie jumped down from the swing and emerged into the afternoon light. 'I'm sorry, Mom,' she apologised. 'I found a swing on this tree and forgot about the time.'

Rose put her arms around her daughter. 'That's all right, dear,' she said, patting her on the back. 'As long as you are happy.'

'You know what, I feel like a child again, as if I knew this house and garden and have come back,' mused Amie.

'This is probably what you need to sort yourself out, to imagine going back to childhood,' explained Rose.

Pulling back the branches and leaves, Rose entered the haven of the tree and exclaimed in her turn on the swing. Amie told her mother to sit on the swing and pushed her gently to and fro.

'See what I mean?' queried Amie.

'This is so relaxing,' agreed Rose.

'A hideout away from the world!' Amie proclaimed. 'No worries or troubles here!'

'Quite so,' Rose said. 'Do you realise we have had nothing to eat, and we have the unpacking to do?'

The two women made their way back along the garden to the house as the setting sun glimmered weakly through the clouds.

Chapter Twenty-Nine

After a good night's sleep, Amie awoke to the glow of the morning sunlight on her amber walls. Slowly remembering where she was, a feeling of contentment encompassed her. There was so much for her to do here. The garden needed some work and she must find the best walks.

Rooting through her wardrobe for some casual clothes, she dug out some jeans and a tee shirt. A look downstairs told her that Rose was not yet awake. Coffee would not take long to make. Amie quickly made some and took a cup up to her mother.

Rose woke up some time later to find a cooling cup of coffee on her bedside table. Amie must have awoken early. There was a whirring, clattering sound outside. From the back window she could see her daughter busily attacking the long grass on the lawn.

Rose sleepily descended the stairs and put the kettle on again. Amie burst in through the back door, wiping her brow.

'Gosh, I'm pooped,' she gasped, flopping into a chair. 'I can't finish that all in one go.'

'You shouldn't try to do too much,' Rose warned. 'Take things easy for a while.'

'I think I'll have a lie down,' agreed Amie.

'I've never seen you do any gardening before,' called Rose after the retreating figure of her daughter.

While Amie was lying down, Rose had a closer inspection of the house. There was a television and a telephone. In a cabinet she found some videos and CDs. The record player was set into the bookcase.

Rose took some coffee upstairs to her daughter, whom she found fast asleep again. Hearing the sound of scampering on the roof, she looked out of the bathroom window. Leaves from the trees were tapping tentatively at the edge of the gutter. With a cheeky twitch of his bushy tail, a grey squirrel leapt agilely into the branches and disappeared from view.

Humming quietly to herself, Rose went to her bedroom to get dressed. This house seemed so friendly and relaxing. There were signs of the previous inhabitant: a jumble of oddments on a bench in the downstairs cloakroom. Among them were a man's mackintosh and boots.

The phone began to ring insistently. Rose hurried into the living room and picked up the receiver. A beloved voice spoke to her. How had George known where she was?

'George, how lovely to hear your voice,' she cried.

'I couldn't wait to speak to you again,' he confessed.

'How did you know where we were?' she asked. 'We only arrived here yesterday.'

'That's a long story,' he replied. 'Henry Brown was told by Fred Martin to let you have that house.'

'Well, I don't know how Wanda's friend could tell our agent about this particular house,' Rose persevered.

'Don't worry now, I'll write you,' George replied soothingly.

'We bought some postcards to send you,' said Rose.

'I look forward to receiving them,' said George.

They said their goodbyes and Rose stared at the wall for a while, her thoughts far away. A knock came at the front door, startling her. A stout elderly woman stood on the doorstep, beaming. A basket was clutched in her chubby hand.

'Hello, dear,' she intoned, genially adjusting her felt hat more firmly on her white curls. 'Mr Brown said to carry on cleaning while you were staying here.'

'Oh', muttered Rose, at a loss for words, 'won't you come in Mrs Er?'

'Just call me Elsie,' the woman commanded, sweeping grandly into the hall and removing her coat. A navy blue frock and white apron were revealed but the hat always stayed on. Rose never saw her without the hat. 'I didn't get here too early in case you were still asleep,' sniffed the woman.

'Do you always clean here?' asked Rose.

'Of course, I have to look after Mr Robert, when he is here,' replied Elsie. 'By the way, do you want to make the tea while I get on?' A sweet smile belied the implied order.

Rose gave in and went into the kitchen to make tea. Elsie took some carpet slippers from her basket and sat on a kitchen chair to put them on.

'I suffer with my feet something awful,' she explained. 'Must be comfy to do my work.' A sudden burst of laughter came from her lips.

Something about her reminded Rose of Ernie, the taxi driver. 'Tell me, Elsie, are you related to Ernie who drove us here from the station?' she asked.

'Our Ernie, my nephew; he's a good lad,' replied Elsie. 'He was brought up in London, but lives here now.'

'Do you all live near the station?' asked Rose.

'No, we live down the lane a way in the hamlet,' said Elsie. 'Now where's my tea? I'm spitting feathers!'

Elsie proved to be a good worker, in spite of her forth-right manner. When she looked in the garden and saw Amie's attempts to cut the grass, she snorted and promised to send 'our Ernie' round to finish the job. Rose asked her to leave the upstairs as her daughter was tired and needed to rest. At that moment the phone rang.

The caller was Henry Brown. 'Hi, Rose, how are you?' he greeted her.

'Hello, Henry,' enthused Rose. 'The house is really wonderful. Amie has simply fallen in love with the place.'

'Great!' said Henry. 'Look, the owner is in the locality, and wants to call in and welcome you to England.'

'I don't see why not,' agreed Rose. 'Do you mean this Mr Robert?'

Elsie's head peered inquisitively round the door.

'Mr Robert?' she repeated excitedly. 'Is he coming here?'

'Wait a minute, Elsie,' Rose said, a little irritated. 'What did you say, Henry?'

'His name is Robert James,' explained Henry. 'Didn't you know?'

'The name sounds vaguely familiar,' admitted Rose. 'Has this something to do with Fred Martin?'

'Well yes,' agreed Henry. 'He said he knew you and this man had offered him his place for Amie's recovery.'

'I see,' said Rose, not really seeing. 'We would be glad.'

Elsie took the phone from her. 'Mr Brown, when is Mr Robert coming here?' she asked.

'This afternoon, I think,' replied Henry.

Elsie put down the phone. 'I'll make a nice cake for you dear. I know what Mr Robert likes with his tea.'

Rose gave up the unequal struggle and let Elsie get on with her arrangements, apart from a mild protest at taking up all of her time. They had a light lunch before the baking began.

There was the question of whether Elsie would stay in the house all day. 'What time do you finish here today?' Rose asked.

'Don't worry, dear,' said Elsie. 'I'm going when Mr Robert gets here.'

The sound of a car engine could be heard approaching down the lane, then there was silence. Rose heard the measured tread of a man's footsteps on the path and then a pause outside. There was a peremptory knock at the door and Robert James stepped into the hall. At that moment Amie appeared at the top of the stairs, sleepily rubbing her eyes, her hair tousled, still wearing the jeans and tee shirt from the morning. There was a long silence as they looked at each other.

Chapter Thirty

Amie felt completely shocked. Having been woken from a deep sleep by the sound of strange voices, she had begun to walk down the stairs and had been confronted by the sight of the last man in the world she expected to see.

Without thinking, she burst out angrily, 'Is this some nightmare? What do I have to do to get away from you?'

Robert James took a deep breath but did not speak. Rose gasped, trying to understand what was going on beneath the surface. Henry Brown entered the doorway just in time to hear those remarks. Elsie bristled and was the first to get her opinion heard.

'How dare you speak to Mr Robert like that? Who do you think you are?'

Robert James turned calmly to Elsie and proceeded to defuse the situation.

'How nice to see you, Elsie. I can smell your baking from here. How delicious! There's nothing to worry about with Mrs Blake, only a little misunderstanding.' So saying, he put his arm comfortingly round the cleaner's ample shoulders and steered her gently but firmly towards the kitchen, telling her everything was going to be all right and suggesting a nice cup of tea all round.

Robert James re-entered the hall, where everyone else was frozen in the same position, uncertain what to say. He turned towards Rose. 'Mrs Collins, I presume. May I say how much I have been looking forward to meeting you?

This might seem strange to you but your daughter and I have met before, socially. You see, I am the owner of this house and when I heard from an acquaintance in America of your circumstances, I was only too pleased to make the facilities available to you.'

He leaned forward easily to shake hands with Rose.

Henry Brown stepped forward from the doorway. 'Hem, I didn't know you ladies had met the owner before,' he said. 'This must have been a surprise to you.'

Rose recovered her composure in order to play the perfect hostess. 'Forgive me, I was confused for a moment. Won't you sit down and join us in some tea, both of you?'

'Very nice. Most acceptable,' said Henry Brown, relieved that the situation seemed to be resolved.

They all looked towards the stairs, to discover that Amie was no longer there. The reason for her quietness was her disappearance to her bedroom to lie in anger and embarrassment, face down on her bed.

Why does he do that? she asked herself harshly. *He creeps about putting me right and making me look a fool. What is he doing here, anyway? That silly amused look in his eyes makes me sick.*

Meanwhile, Rose was putting the guests at their ease. Elsie entered the room, beaming again and carrying a tray of tea. Having deposited that on the coffee table, she returned to the kitchen and reappeared almost at once with a sponge cake, resting on a paper lace doily on a plate. True to her word, she then left quietly.

Rose apologised for leaving her guests and slipped upstairs to check on Amie. Looking into the room, she found her daughter lying face down with her head under the pillow. Slowly her fists pounded the mattress one by one. A muffled groaning came from the vicinity of her face.

'Amie, what in heaven's name is wrong with you?' Rose whispered urgently. 'Do you know that man, and what has he done to you?'

'Can't you leave me alone?' came the muffled reply. 'Won't you all leave me alone?'

Rose patted her on the back and returned downstairs. Forcing a smile as she descended the stairs, she walked to the coffee table to pour out the tea.

'I'm sorry about that,' she said. 'Amie is still not herself and must have been startled, waking up suddenly like that.'

'No, I'm the one who should apologise,' insisted Robert. 'My actions were thoughtless. I assumed you knew this was my house. Now I understand you do not know me from Adam.'

'You say you met Amie in America,' remarked Rose. 'I don't remember her mentioning you.'

'I was there briefly,' said Robert, lightly. 'I worked with someone who knew her and we bumped into each other a few times.'

'How did you know she was ill?' persisted Rose.

'When I rang, someone mentioned her accident and Fred Martin asked whether I knew of a holiday home in England,' replied Robert.

He was becoming tired of justifying himself. Henry thought the atmosphere was becoming tense and, being more sensitive than he looked, saved the day.

'Come along,' he said. 'Now how about some of Elsie's delicious cake. We'll never be forgiven if every scrap is not eaten.'

The two men stayed with Rose, talking to her for a short time. Then Robert looked at his watch and announced he must leave. Henry Brown leapt to his feet and held the door open for his companion. The tall, thin man nodded at Rose and stooped to avoid hitting his head on the lintel as he left.

What a strange man! Rose said to herself as she began carrying the tea things into the kitchen.

There was a sharp rap on the door and Robert looked into the hall. 'By the way,' he said. 'Tell Mrs Blake not to worry. Won't be around for a while. We're off to the Continent next week so shan't be worrying you again.' He raised his tweed trilby and left.

'Did he hear me say that,' Rose asked herself. If only George were here. These English were peculiar.

From outside, Henry Brown could be heard, calling, 'Goodbye, Rose.'

Later on, Rose took a bowl of soup and some sandwiches up to Amie. The young woman was kneeling on the window seat, gazing out at the window at the garden. The day was drawing towards evening. Ernie's promised sun had made an appearance but the two women had not been out for long: too much had been happening.

'Do you want to tell me about this man?' Rose asked her daughter. 'What has he done to you?'

'He has done nothing,' replied Amie irritably. 'When I met him he was John Peters' friend, who always seemed to be there.'

After this she shut up like a clam and declined to talk about him. However, she showed some interest when Rose disclosed that Robert was going away to the Continent for some time and so would not trouble her. Why should he think he troubled her? What the heck was he doing lending them a country house anyway?

'Mom, I think we should find another place,' said Amie that night.

'I thought you liked this one so much, and so do I!' objected Rose.

'I feel like an object of pity and charity,' Amie complained.

'I am sure Robert does not think like that and this does not seem to be his main house,' Rose assured her.

Robert and Henry had told Rose of various walks that she and Amie could take. Perhaps they could start exploring in the morning. They would be able to go farther if they hired a car. Amie muttered a half agreement.

So these were all Robert's possessions in this house. Strange that Amie had felt an affinity with the person who lived here; as if she already knew them. So, of course, she did – a little, anyway. Looking through the videos for films to view that night, she found that they had much the same taste in topics, too.

That man always seems to be looking over my shoulder, even when he is not here, came the thought, unbidden, into her head. *What must he have thought of my outburst this afternoon?*

Chapter Thirty-One

After this the weeks went by uneventfully. Rose and Amie discovered the nearby hamlet of Barfield, where Elsie, Ernie and the rest of their family lived. Barfield was situated down the lane, in the opposite direction from the station. Nestling among the cottages was a small hostelry, The King's Head.

The King's Head was the local meeting place. Rose and Amie took to walking there at lunchtime or in the evening for a quiet drink. They became quite used to English cider and beer. Between the rear of the pub and an old orchard was a garden furnished with rough-hewn tables and chairs, where the customers could relax with a pint and breathe in the fresh country air.

When the two women had first appeared in the Lounge Bar of The King's Head, the landlord, Barney, already knew their names and where they were staying – Mr Robert's place. Apparently they were deemed privileged to be allowed to stay in his house, although Amie was convinced odd looks were directed her way behind her back.

Mr Robert James must be a pretty important person round here, Amie thought to herself with irritation.

At first, the two women were put out by the interest shown in their private affairs. Before long they came to be accepted by the locals and were not too worried by them.

Rose was honoured by being invited to visit Elsie's mother, who lived in a little cottage with her daughter.

When they arrived for the visit, the old lady was sitting in her rocking chair in the sun-dappled doorway, her old tabby cat dozing on her lap.

'I've brought Mrs Collins to see you,' Elsie said loudly in her mother's ear. 'Staying in Mr Robert's little place they are.'

As Rose shook the old woman's hand, she wondered yet again why everyone spoke of Mr Robert James with such reverence; he must be the landlord. Elsie was certainly very short with Amie, ever since she snubbed the man when they first arrived there.

Elsie's mother nodded and grinned, showing her tooth-less gums. The old woman stood up and deposited the cat on the cushion of the rocking chair. 'To keep me seat warm,' she said, chortling. With dogged determination, she shuffled through the doorway as fast as her legs and age would allow. The sound of the kettle being filled and placed on the hob, came from the interior.

'Should we help her?' asked Rose, anxiously.

'Don't need no help. Very stubborn, my mother. Keeps her going that does. Be offended, she would, if anyone tried to take over when company is here,' warned Elsie.

Rose nodded her agreement and seated herself on the wooden bench, positioned against the white-washed cottage wall. Honeysuckle and roses cast their scent carelessly on the summer afternoon breeze, as bumble-bees droned steadily amongst the blooms. A quaint old broom, made from twigs tied to a handle, propped up by the door. Elsie sighed and eased her ample frame down alongside her visitor.

'What a swell place for retirement,' Rose mused.

'We don't retire in the country,' remonstrated Elsie tartly.

They were called indoors by the old woman, who had served tea in flowered china cups on a snowy linen tablecloth and biscuits on a china stand. The room was spick and span, with a black leaded range in the chimney nook and shiny brown porcelain dogs on the mantelpiece. Wild flowers were arranged in a bright blue glass vase on the table. When the ladies had finished their tea, and Rose made ready to leave, she said how much she had enjoyed herself, pleasing her hostess very much.

'Remember me to Mr Robert, won't you,' mumbled the old woman, leaning heavily on her stick as she ushered her guest to the cottage doorway.

'Your mother is wonderful,' enthused Rose, as Elsie walked to the white wicket garden gate with her.

'Fourteen children she's had, six still living,' boasted Elsie.

'Gosh!' exclaimed Rose. 'Do they all live near here?'

'Hereabouts, farming and stuff,' disclosed Elsie.

'Say, Elsie', Rose asked, changing the subject, 'what does this Mr Robert do? I wondered why everyone talks about him as if he were important. Is he the landlord?'

'My dear, I thought you knew!' Elsie exclaimed. 'We thought you were friends of his. He only lets his friends stay in that house. He is the landlord not only of this place, but of all around here: he is the Lord of the Manor.'

'He's a real lord?' gasped Rose. 'Are you positive about this?'

'As sure as I'm standing here,' affirmed Elsie. 'His father, the Viscount, passed on a few months ago and, as eldest son, Mr Robert had to come back here from America, to take over his responsibilities.'

Rose just stood there, muttering, 'Oh my gosh, we didn't know. After all Amie has said to him...!'

Elsie patted Rose's hand, comfortingly. 'There, my dear. He is a lovely man, who won't bear no grudges.'

'Where does he live, then?' asked Rose in bewilderment.

'Why, up at the big house, some way off,' replied Elsie. So saying, she walked back up the path, shaking her head pityingly.

Rose hurried back down the lane towards their house, where Amie had been resting in the garden. Of course, everything now fell into place. The respect, and even awe, in the local inhabitants' voices when they spoke of him, and their behaviour when they met him was all explained. The feudal system in England held him in high regard, and so did visiting American tourists.

Rose hurried into the house and called Amie, who emerged from the bathroom, wrapped in a towel.

'Have a nice visit, Mom?' she asked.

'Never mind that,' Rose replied.

'Why, what's wrong with you?' asked Amie, following her mother into her bedroom.

'Get yourself dressed,' Rose requested. 'I have something to tell you.'

'You sound worried, Mom,' Amie called from her bedroom as she pulled on a shirt and slacks. 'Has something happened to Poppy?' Her voice rose in alarm. She rushed into Rose's bedroom.

'Of course Poppy is well,' Rose assured her daughter. 'You would know anything like that before me, anyway.'

'Yes,' agreed Amie. 'Poppy only rang me last night.'

Rose sat on her bed and patted the space next to her for Amie to sit down. 'I have been told something today.'

Amie sat next to her mother, becoming impatient. 'Stop being mysterious; what is this something?'

'Robert James,' said Rose. 'Didn't you notice anything strange about him?'

'Well, yes,' agreed Amie. 'I can't help liking him, though, in spite of everything.'

'Elsie tells me he is the lord of everything here, for miles around,' declared Rose. 'He lives in a big house, which he inherited from his father a few months ago, and he is a viscount.'

'So that is why he suddenly left America to come back here,' mused Amie in a flat, unemotional tone. 'I wondered where he had gone.'

Strange that she was not really surprised. Relief was her main reaction that he had not gone away and left her without good cause when she had most needed him. He had written to her after all. Robert had to come back to England where his duty lay but Amie felt she could not explain her regret of her treatment of him, after her recent rebuff of him.

Chapter Thirty-Two

In order to enjoy their stay in England, the two women had arranged to visit London to see the sights. This they decided to do, in order to take their minds off the recent events. They were to book into a modest hotel, see the city's landmarks and visit the theatre.

Therefore, before too much time had passed, Rose and Amie went up to London. They stayed a few days and visited the usual sights: Buckingham Palace, the Tower of London, Trafalgar Square and Tower Bridge. Then came the art galleries and museums, not forgetting St. Paul's Cathedral and Westminster Abbey.

Within a short space of time they were loaded down with carrier bags of mementoes and postcards.

'Poppy is going to love these pictures and cute little dolls dressed as guardsmen,' enthused Rose.

Even Amie became interested in seeing the lovely old city. Seeing all the historic buildings made her puny little life seem unimportant by comparison. As she sat with her mother in one of the beautiful parks, feeding the ducks and other birds, thoughts of the history and tradition stretching back into the distant past drifted though her mind. Robert James must feel strongly about his heritage and the obligations handed on to him from past generations.

'Let's go back to the hotel,' said Amie, leaping to her feet and walking away briskly.

'What is the hurry and why were you smiling to your-self?' asked Rose, hastening after the retreating figure of her daughter.

'I was thinking about history,' was Amie's enigmatic reply.

There was to be a theatre party that evening. Getting ready for an outing can be almost as exciting as the actual event. The beauty parlour was honoured by a visit from the pair. Hair, skin, nails and eyes received attention; then the two women dressed in cocktail length outfits and set off for their meeting place.

As they stepped into the taxi, Rose looked at Amie and told her she looked lovely in her gold lace frock. Amie told Rose that she, too, looked ravishing in her lilac silk gown.

'A pity we have no men with us to admire us,' commented Rose.

'Yes, a pity about men,' agreed Amie.

They dined at an Indian restaurant with some friends of Henry Brown and Fred Martin. The company was pleasant enough. Several middle-aged couples made up the group. Soon they had relaxed and talking together in a friendly fashion.

Rose had secretly hoped that there would be a suitable younger man for Amie, but hid her disappointment admirably. The party was made up of both English and Americans, so there was plenty to discuss. All too soon the time came for the transfer to the theatre. Their host and his wife went in one taxi with the two women, and the others followed in another.

During the short drive to the theatre, they discussed the musical show they were about to see. 'This is the first show we have seen in London,' said Rose. 'We feel quite excited.'

'Yes, surely,' agreed Amie.

'I am sure you are going to enjoy yourself,' said their host, Samuel Goodman, a handsome white-haired man with an authoritative manner. He peered out of the taxi window. 'Ah, here we are.'

They drew up at the kerb outside the theatre. 'Come along, my dears,' ordered Sam's wife, Sarah, easing her slim figure out of the taxi. 'Follow me and you won't get lost.'

A uniformed doorman had stepped forward to open the taxi door. He smiled and touched his peaked cap to the ladies.

'He's rather cute, you know,' remarked Rose.

'Mother!' whispered Amie in a shocked voice.

'Don't worry, dear, he loves all that,' said Sarah.

The doorman grinned broadly and looked back over his shoulder at them.

Another man opened the glass doors to the theatre for the group. As they walked into the foyer, Amie whispered fiercely into her mother's ear. 'Why did you act like that with him. This is not like you!'

'Must have been the wine,' said Rose. 'Anyway this is a bit of role reversal here, with you acting like my maiden aunt, for goodness sake!'

The group of theatregoers waited a few minutes for the other members of their party to arrive. Sam remarked, 'Well, my children, we have a box for tonight.' There were general murmurs of approval from the guests. Then the complement of their party burst into the foyer in a colourful, chattering flock.

When they were ready, an usherette led the way upstairs and along a corridor, lined crimson plush-lined. Pulling back one of the curtains, the woman directed them into the box. There was a marvellous view of the stage. Only now, of course this was obscured by the magnificent red and gold patterned curtain.

Above them was the elaborately ornamented ceiling, bordered with gilt cherubs, glancing cheekily down at the audience. Rose and Amie sat warily on the fragile-looking chairs provided in the box. The curving edge in front of them was padded with soft red velvet. Above their heads, a myriad of tiny lights twinkled down from rows of chandeliers.

The atmosphere in a theatre just before the performance begins brings a tinge of anticipation to even the dullest mind. The starling-like chatter of the patrons and the whisper of silks and satins as ladies seat themselves, punctuated by the staccato sound of sharply rustling programme pages, make the pizzicato on the background of the humming noise a multitude makes just being together.

Then the lights began to dim, imperceptibly at first. The auditorium became dark. Only little pinpricks of light remained in the black velvet of the ceiling. All eyes were turned towards the proscenium.

The lights came up in the orchestra pit. Muted sounds of instruments being tuned floated jerkily through the gloom. As always, at this point there was a rash of coughing. Then silence as the mighty curtain crept steadily upwards.

Rose enjoyed the show but secretly wished George could be there to share the experience with her. Out of the corner of her eye, she could see Amie sitting motionless next to her at the end of the row of chairs. No use wondering how she felt; sometimes she hid her feelings beneath a frosty exterior.

The musical show was colourful and melodic. The main theme was the guy got the girl after lots of misunderstandings and adventures. Unlike real life, thought Rose. There were fixtures on the box rail containing little binoculars for their use, and they amused themselves looking at the expressions on the artists' faces: some wore fixed smiles and others gazed far into the distance.

As Amie sat there, not thinking, just being, she became aware that the curtain behind her was moving. Someone was pulling the folds apart. The darkness made vision impossible. Quiet, stealthy movements continued until she was aware of a presence behind her.

Then a chair was put almost silently through the curtain and the someone sat down, muttering an almost imperceptible 'Thank you'. Who could this be, coming into their box? Surely all of their party were already present. Amie would look round when the lights went up at the end of the first act.

The feeling of eyes examining the back of her head began to irritate Amie. Beginning to feel awkward, she fidgeted with her purse. At last the lights went up again and she quickly turned her head. There, right behind her, was Robert James.

'Oh!' was all Amie could say.

Robert leaned towards her, conspiratorially. 'So sorry to have startled you. Afraid I arrived late and didn't want to spoil the performance.' He spoke in a low voice, a slight smile playing round the edge of his mouth.

'I didn't know you were going to be here,' hissed Amie in annoyance. 'I thought you were abroad.'

'Yes, on business for a while,' said Robert. 'Now I am back, but I told Sam not to say anything in case I was delayed.'

Chapter Thirty-Three

'Ah, there you are Robert,' came Sam's voice from the far side of the box. 'Pity you missed the first act, but quite frankly you didn't miss much, and we can bring you up to date over a drink in the bar.'

Robert stood up and offered Amie his hand. He led her from the box.

Rose followed them closely. 'I wondered who you were whispering to, Amie,' she remarked. 'Did you know Mr James was coming here tonight?'

'No, I did not,' retorted Amie sharply. 'This was as much a surprise to me as to you.'

Robert smiled. 'Forgive me, both of you, for the suddenness of my arrival. Sam made up the party and I told him to say nothing in case I could not attend.'

He offered an arm to each lady and escorted them to the bar. The others in their party were already there and soon the noise in the crowded room made conversation almost impossible. Rose soon cheered up with a martini in her hand. Amie sipped some mineral water and gazed thoughtfully at the sepia photographs on the wall.

Robert was standing close to her, under pressure from the crowd. 'Are you sure that is all you want?' he asked in her ear.

'Yes, I had wine at dinner and want to keep a clear head,' Amie said loudly back at him.

Robert raised a quizzical eyebrow. Amie could not help admiring his appearance in evening clothes. The subtle aroma of his aftershave came faintly to her. He was taller than she remembered as he looked down with that crooked smile of his.

'I must apologise for standing so near', he mouthed, 'the crowd, you know.'

Amie was beginning to feel uncomfortable. His body, although tall and thin, was also muscular and, finding herself responding to his warmth, she had to prevent herself from leaning against him.

'I want to ask you something,' she almost shouted.

'Later,' said Robert. 'Too noisy and crowded in here.'

Fortunately the bell for the next act sounded and the party extricated themselves from the throng in order to return to their box. Amie caught her mother frowning at her and several of the other guests smiled and nodded at her. One of the men even winked. What was the matter with them?

Surely the fact that she had been forced to stand close to Robert James had not given them the wrong impression. Perhaps they all knew he was a viscount. The man was becoming a nuisance. He was causing her all sorts of problems.

Firstly there was his attitude of watching over her and waiting for her to do something stupid so that he could patronise her. Secondly, he seemed to appear out of the blue at any given moment. Thirdly, he made her feel inept and clumsy. Fourthly, he made her feel ashamed of her unusually bad manners towards him, which he fended off in a good-natured manner. Fifthly, there was his inheritance, which he had not seen fit to mention. Sixthly, he had hurt her by leaving America for England, just after her accident, although she knew now why he had to go.

If Robert were only to answer back and reply to her barbed comments, she would be happier. If he would explain his feelings to her, perhaps they could be friends. Amie had become used to his being there to help her in adversity. For some time she had driven to the back of her mind the memory of his anxious face peering in the car window at her after that accident; now all her memories of that day came flooding back.

Amie turned her head to look sharply up at him as they reached the curtained doorway to their box. He looked down with a frown and drew her aside to let the others enter the box first.

'Why, what is the matter?' Robert asked her abruptly, his hand holding her wrist tightly. 'You look at me so hostilely.' His eyes had become hard and steely and he seemed a different man.

'Nothing is wrong so let me go!' exclaimed Amie. 'I was just remembering, I never thanked you for saving my life.' Tears welled up in her eyes; tears that had remained unshed for weeks.

Robert held both of her hands tenderly. 'Is that all that look was? I was frightened that you hated me.'

'Of course I don't hate you,' replied Amie. 'I thought you pitied me.'

'Let's slip away afterwards and we can sort this out,' suggested Robert.

'Yes, I think we have to,' replied Amie artlessly.

Robert drew the curtain back and Amie slipped inside. The second act had already begun and heads turned curiously as they found their seats. Music and songs flowed unheard around her as she tried to get her thoughts in order. What had happened out there?

Amie hoped she had not made a fool of herself again. Robert had been in her background for what seemed like ages and she had never put him in perspective. They must discuss this like adults. When her concerns were sorted out she would return to America.

The rest of the programme washed over Amie like the waves of dreamless sleep. Behind her sat Robert, and she could feel his eyes on her. Turning halfway round, she hissed, 'Stop staring at me.' He leaned forward and whispered in her ear, 'I'm not staring at you,' but she knew he was lying.

The second interval was a nightmare. Her mother questioned Amie on what she and Robert were discussing.

'That man saved my life,' replied Amie. 'Surely I can have a conversation with him.'

Rose was taken aback and went to have another drink. How she was missing George! The day must soon dawn when she could get back to him. When she arrived back at the hotel that night, she would sit down and write to him, telling him how much she missed him. In the meantime Amie and Robert continued to talk earnestly in corners; what was up with those two?

The rest of the programme staggered to a close. Apparently the critics agreed with the audience; the musical play was a flop. A contrite Sam apologised to the others for booking tickets to such a fiasco.

'Nonsense,' said Robert as they left the theatre. 'This was a lovely evening and we must take these guests of ours to another show before their visit here draws to a close.'

Robert escorted Rose and Amie to their hotel. In the second act interval he had confessed that he had a room there also. Adieux were exchanged with the other guests. They were going on to a nightclub.

As Rose felt a bit the worse for wear, Amie took her up to their room and left her scribbling a letter to George. After kissing her mother goodnight, the young woman went straight out again. Robert was waiting for her down in the foyer.

Robert took her hand in his. 'At last we can have that talk,' he said, smiling warmly. Amie responded by squeezing his hand as they left the hotel for the dark street.

They walked in the park where she had fed the ducks. They had long since nested for the night. The trees loomed strangely in the gloom. In the dark were other couples, silhouetted against the night sky.

'Where can we go to talk?' asked Amie. 'Somewhere we can sit opposite each other and just discuss things. I don't know why. I need to ask you about the past and what makes you tick.'

'I, too, would like to delve into your mind,' replied Robert. 'You are the most complicated, infuriating, changeable and lovely woman I have ever known.'

He turned her to face him and, under the shadow of a tree, he leaned down to kiss her gently on her mouth. His lips were gentle, the skin on them dry as they brushed gently to and fro on hers. After a minute he straightened up. A groan came from the depths of his soul.

Chapter Thirty-Four

'What is the matter?' asked Amie, breathlessly.

'You don't know how long I have wanted to do that,' Robert gasped. 'I am only flesh and blood, you know.'

'I feel such a fool,' whispered Amie as she drew his head towards her. 'I thought you despised me, always correcting me.'

Placing her mouth on his, she kissed him back.

'Oh, wonderful,' he said quietly.

'That was for saving me,' she said. 'Now where can we have that talk?'

Robert laughed and put his arm round her shoulders. 'I know just the place,' he said and started to lead her towards the lights on the main road.

'Robert', said Amie, 'you have had fun and smiled more tonight than I have ever seen. You always seemed such a solemn man.'

'Haven't you realised Amie,' asked Robert, 'I have been madly in love with you from the first moment I saw you, and this is the first night you have been so near to me? In the theatre bar I could feel your breath on my chin. In the box I could look at you, silhouetted against the brightly-lit stage.'

'Wait a minute here,' Amie protested. 'This is the first reference you have made to love.' In the dark she could feel her face reddening in confusion.

'Forgive me,' Robert begged, stopping on the path and holding her at arm's length. 'I am rushing you. But I was so relieved to kiss you at last, and feel your body against mine.'

'You always seemed so superior, watching me from a distance,' said Amie, bemused. 'You looked down on me with your amused detachment.'

'That must have been shyness,' Robert replied. 'You were very much involved with, erm, someone else – and all I could do was warn you, which did not meet with much success!'

They had continued walking, and by this time had reached a little café, more like a shack, with the name 'Vinny's Diner' in scripted fluorescent-tubing letters on the outside, by the road. Robert pushed open the door and ushered Amie inside. A plump, sleepy-eyed man, wearing dark trousers and a broad-striped shirt with the sleeves rolled up to display his tattoos; the lot covered by a rough cotton apron and the ensemble topped by a natty bow tie, was reading his paper behind the counter. The rickety tables in the cafe were covered with brightly coloured check tablecloths.

Robert and Amie glanced at each other. 'The same colour as in the place we met when you warned me about, erm, something,' Amie said, in a mock-teasing manner.

'You were wearing a pretty little turquoise sweater,' Robert reminded her.

'Fancy your remembering that!' said Amie, astonished.

'Shall we sit down,' Robert said, ushering her to a table. 'Would you like coffee?'

The proprietor brought them over two cups of fresh coffee, and they sat, opposite each other, sipping the hot fragrance appreciatively. Amie picked up a fork and began to draw lines on the yellow checked tablecloth with the prongs. Outside, the intermittent noise of traffic and the glare of occasional headlights reflected on the wall, punctuated their conversation. Robert rested his elbows on the table and gazed into the girl's eyes as he stroked his moustache.

'You did that last time we sat in a café together,' said Amie.

'And you drew lines on the cloth,' retorted Robert.

'And you left in a huff with my paying the bill,' replied Amie.

'Oh, did I really?' asked Robert. 'Forgive me, but you annoyed me.'

'I was ungrateful after you tried to warn me about John Peters,' Amie agreed. 'Yet you turned out to be right.'

'Look, when I first met you at the swimming party, I could see you had eyes for no one else but him,' Robert explained. 'What could a poor old foreigner like me do to attract your attention?'

'I thought you found us extremely boring,' Amie remarked.

'I remember retreating behind my pipe,' Robert explained. 'Something to do with my hands while you were next to me.'

'Did you really like me then?' the girl persisted. 'You seemed so distant, as though you did not belong.'

'We English do not carry our hearts on our sleeves,' said the man. 'Yet we can be truly faithful.'

'What a lovely thought,' said Amie.

'May I?' Robert asked, reaching across the table and holding her hand gently in his, before continuing his story. 'At that point I was uncertain what to do. John did not, of course, know how I felt about you, so he spoke openly about his feelings. I knew he would never give up Joanne Webber as his fiancée, as she was Bill Webber, the film producer's, sister; good connections, you know!'

'He told me that was nothing serious,' Amie protested. 'I thought that was finished!'

'Then', Robert continued, 'he told me of your visits to the cabin and how, sorry to repeat this, exciting you were.'

Amie took her hand from his and covered her hot face. 'You make me sound like a—' she began.

Robert retrieved her hand and kissed her palm lightly. 'Nonsense. I knew he was deceiving you and was going to let you go that day of the rain on the mountain. He was my friend so I did not know what to do. Trying to be there for you seemed to irritate you. Trying to warn you looked like interference. Did you know, by the way, that the cabin belonged to Bill Webber? John only borrowed the keys, and Joanne found out.'

'So she knew all the time!' exclaimed Amie. 'What a little fool I must have seemed. I thought I was safe in my own secret world. Yet all the time everyone was watching me and making comments. Even my mother was trying to warn me.'

'John thought he would enjoy himself whilst his fiancée was away, you know, while the cat's away the mice will play...' said Robert. 'I wanted to help you without appearing, what do you say, pushy.'

'My work suffered and I feel I let down my little daughter,' said Amie.

'Don't blame yourself for what someone else does,' said Robert. 'You were in a vulnerable position and John took advantage of you.'

'So, how did you happen to appear like an angel at the car window when I needed you?' Amie asked.

'How nice to hear you needed me,' Robert smiled broadly. 'Well, I knew John had taken you up the mountain to the cabin for the weekend and I was madly jealous and also worried for you, as he had told me he would let you go after that. Then the weather forecasts were bad: heavy rain. When I rang his flat the next day, when he should have been back, there was no reply, so I alerted the police. They called out the emergency services. There had been land-slides on the mountains and the roads were bad. Naturally I drove up there first to see what I could do. The road had collapsed on a corner and there was the car, way down the slope, wedged against a tree. If that tree had not been there, things might have been much worse.'

Robert paused for breath and Amie walked to the counter and ordered more coffee. The proprietor emerged from behind his paper to refill their cups. 'Sandwiches?' he asked. They rather thought they would. 'Cheese and pickle, ham, egg or tuna salad?' he asked. They ordered and ate their sandwiches and, taking sips of hot coffee, returned to their conversation.

Chapter Thirty-Five

'Then what happened when you saw the car?' continued Amie.

'A helicopter was flying overhead and an ambulance was at the edge of the gaping hole where the road had been. I asked to be allowed to climb down as I was a friend of the car's occupants. They might be pleased to see a friendly face.'

'I certainly was pleased to see you after that night of being trapped in the car,' interjected Amie.

'The medics tied a rope to me,' continued Robert. 'We had done some rock-climbing at school and in the army so I knew what to do. I went down carefully, trying not to displace any more of the mud. When I reached the car window I looked in and saw your pale, dirty face peering out at me. Tears were running down your cheeks. They were worth more than diamonds, as they showed you were still with me. I thanked God you were alive. Then I checked John and he was unconscious, but breathing evenly.'

Robert was clutching Amie's hand tightly. The incident was obviously still vivid in his mind and he needed to talk the occurrence through as much as she did. He looked into her eyes, a frown creasing his forehead. They were both silent for a while.

'So you were a hero!' Amie exclaimed.

'No, I was in no danger.' Robert dismissed his exploits self-deprecatingly. 'I was only worried for you. I gave you a sip of water and told you not to swallow, as the ambulance man had told me. You passed out, and with the help of the emergency services and the helicopter, you were both removed to hospital.'

'I have never talked this accident through with anyone,' Amie confessed. 'Have you?'

'No, I would not discuss you, or your affairs, with anyone,' Robert replied gallantly. 'I think we both needed to talk.'

'Even your face at the car window,' said Amie. 'That picture has been at the back of my mind but never in my consciousness. At times I thought I must have imagined you. Then, when you failed to visit me, I was strangely hurt and pushed the image from my mind.'

'Unfortunately, when I arrived back at my flat there was bad news,' Robert replied. 'My father had passed on suddenly and I had to return to England to console my mother and to sort out the arrangements. There was this other business, too. I did not know how matters stood between you and John; I had done my best for you and decided to keep out of the way.'

'You need not have bothered,' said Amie. 'John was down the passage from me in the hospital and never came to see me. Joanne came to my hospital room and accused me of blackmailing John into taking me away for that weekend. I told her to leave. I was planning to go to his room when an orderly brought a note, asking me to visit him. When I went in his room, he was sitting there in plaster and bandages. I told him about Joanne and he admitted he was marrying her and told me our relationship was just one of those things. Can you imagine how I felt? I don't suppose you can.'

'We men have feelings as well,' Robert countered. 'We're not all like that: I really wanted to visit you. Also, I sent you a card.'

'Oh, yes,' Amie smiled. 'I still have your red roses and pink ribbon card and your postcards from England!'

'You kept them, did you?' Robert said, pleased. 'Although you didn't reply, that is not until later.'

'I was not up to anything like that,' Amie replied. 'I asked my mother to take me home. On the way out from hospital, we walked past John, in his wheelchair, being pushed by Joanne. They walked right past us as if we were not there. I felt sick and thought my life was finished.'

'Don't say that, Amie,' Robert murmured, squeezing her hand.

'When I arrived home I couldn't eat or sleep,' Amie continued sombrely. 'I could only cry and have nightmares. My doctor sent me back into hospital. He said I had a nervous breakdown.' Unchecked tears began to trickle down her cheeks.

Robert handed Amie his handkerchief and she dabbed at her face. 'I heard some of this, of course,' he explained. 'I wanted to know how you were. Then I sent the postcards. I hoped you might come to England, and here you are.'

Amie had brightened up. 'You planned all this,' she accused. 'That we would come here and stay in your charming house. You know, I loved that house as soon as I went inside. There is so much character!'

'Thank you,' said Robert. 'That makes everything worthwhile.'

'We did not know you are a viscount,' said Amie. 'Why didn't you tell us?'

'There didn't seem much point,' explained Robert. 'My father could have lived for years yet. He was not old, and I was just an honourable; the eldest son. My inheritance was something that lay far in the future.'

'That is our story, up to today,' said Amie. 'Shall we be friends now? I don't know why I was so hurt you went away. You were someone I thought I could depend upon even though I was not nice to you.'

'Let us forget the past and think of the future,' said Robert. Taking Amie's hand, he stood up to leave. 'Goodness gracious, two o'clock!' he exclaimed, looking at his watch. 'We had better pay the man,' he said, leading the way to the counter.

Robert handed a ten-pound note to the proprietor, who had emerged, running his fingers through his grey-streaked black wavy hair, from his reverie behind the same newspaper to take the money. He waved away the change. The man said to Robert, 'Thanks, guv,' and to Amie, 'that's all right, luv, I hear everything in here,' and winked broadly as they went out.

Laughing together, they walked away arm in arm. There came the sound of bolts being closed on the inside of the door. They turned to see the lights go out, leaving the building in darkness. Amie looked up at Robert.

'He was waiting to close,' she said.

'Perhaps he didn't want to interrupt us,' he said.

'Do you think he was listening to us?' she asked.

'Could have been, but that doesn't matter,' he answered reassuringly. 'What matters now is that we have talked the past through and that barrier has gone down between us. Now we can get to know each other, if you have no objection.'

'Things aren't as simple as that,' said Amie.

'Never mind, look out for a taxi,' said Robert.

'We could walk from here,' said Amie.

'If we see a taxi, we shall ride in style to the hotel,' said Robert.

They did catch a stray cab cruising the deserted streets. Amie found that her legs were tired and she sank back gratefully into the cushioned seat. Robert encouraged her to lean against his shoulder. In a few minutes they were back at the hotel. Outside her room, he kissed her.

'Goodnight,' she whispered.

'You have made me very happy tonight,' he replied.

He walked to the end of the corridor, waved, and ran up the staircase to the next floor. His long legs ate up the distance and soon he was in his room, gazing from the window at the pre-dawn greyness in the sky. Things had certainly changed. Hopeful plans he had made had come to fruition and he had spent an evening, a night even, with the girl who had filled his every waking thought for the greater part of a year.

Robert was surprised at himself. He had never spoken so long or so frankly to anyone before. The air had needed to be cleared, however; though not even his closest friends would have accused him of being an extrovert.

In her room downstairs, Amie collapsed into her bed and fell instantly into a dreamless sleep. Not for a long while had she felt so cleansed and untroubled. That talk had done her good. This Robert was some guy and she was glad he was there to support her.

Rose slept on in the other bed. Her dreams were of George. As yet, she had no idea of the events of the night. When she did, she would be rather bewildered.

Chapter Thirty-Six

Rose and Amie returned to Beech View, the house in Sussex the next day. When they awoke that morning they discovered that Robert had left the hotel early. The two women had their breakfast and left, not speaking much. A note had arrived from Sam and Sarah, mentioning that they hoped to meet the mother and daughter again.

'That was good of them,' said Rose.

The journey back was quiet and uneventful. When they arrived at the front door in Ernie's cab, which had been waiting for them at the station, Elsie was indoors, hat on, cleaning. 'I heard you was coming back, so I thought I'd air the place,' she explained.

'Guess you know everything, Elsie,' remarked Amie, putting her case down in the hall.

'No mystery,' sniffed Elsie. 'They give me a call at The Kings Head from the station.' Elsie still had not forgiven Amie for being sharp with Mr Robert.

'How is your lovely mother?' enquired Rose, bringing up the rear with her case. 'I have brought her a present from London.'

'That's nice of you, dear,' Elsie blew her nose loudly, overcome by emotion. Amie handed her a little bag, containing a silk scarf. 'Oh, she'll love that.'

Elsie bustled into the kitchen to make the tea. 'By the way, dear, there's a gentleman staying at The King's Head. Handsome, he is, and says he knows you,' she called out.

Rose and Amie looked at each other. To whom was she speaking?

'What is his name?' asked Rose, following Elsie into the kitchen.

'He has some foreign name,' said Elsie, disapprovingly, studying the toes of her carpet slippers. 'George Lester something or other.'

'George Lestrange!' cried Rose. 'Amie, George has come to see me.'

'Who's he then, love?' enquired Elsie, pouring out the tea.

'He is my fiancé from America,' explained Rose.

'Fiancé?' came Amie's voice from behind her. 'I didn't know you were engaged! Mother, when did this happen? Why didn't you tell me?'

Rose led Amie into the living room. 'Listen,' she said, holding her daughter by the shoulders. 'You were too ill to be told anything like that. My main concern has been to get you on your feet and to make you better. Poppy needs you and that is important. I can do what I want afterwards.'

'I thought he was just one of your friends,' said Amie. 'I never imagined you would want to get married again.'

'Well, he isn't,' said Rose. 'I am a grown woman and have my own life to lead.'

'I'm going now, love,' called Elsie, going past the door. 'I'll get our Ernie to cut that grass, grown something terrible after all that rain this week.' The front door clicked shut decisively and she was gone.

'I suppose that is going the rounds now,' commented Amie.

'I don't care about that,' said Rose. 'After all I have done for you, you object to my having a man friend!'

Amie threw her arms round Rose. 'Of course I am pleased for you,' she said soothingly. 'You have been wonderful to me and I have been selfish.'

Rose patted her daughter on the back. 'I'm being silly, don't worry. Now, George is here and I must ring him.'

Rose picked up the phone and was soon through to The King's Head. 'George, how wonderful,' she enthused. 'Elsie said you were here. The cleaner. Everyone knows me here. Yes, Amie is fine. How are you, dear? Do you know, I was only writing to you last night and here you are. Stay there and we'll walk down to you. No, not too far. We have just this minute arrived back from London. So long, see you soon.'

Amie was standing by the door, a baffled look on her face. 'You do surprise me,' she said. 'I did not know you were this serious.'

Rose turned to leave the room. 'Not as much as you often surprise me,' she retorted. 'You forget parents are human, too. Come on. We're going to meet George.'

Rose hurried from the house, Amie in tow. They walked briskly down to The King's Head in Barfield. The countryside seemed fresher and greener after their absence, the air cool and invigorating. Soon the hamlet came into sight.

Rose walked into The King's Head. Descending the stairs was the tall, silver-haired figure of George, ducking his head to avoid the beams.

'Honeybun!' he said, grasping Rose's hands in his. 'I saw you from my window up there.'

'How long have you been here?' she asked. 'You remember Amie, don't you,' as her daughter followed her in the door.

'Hi, we have met, before,' George said, 'Let's sit down.'

An interested audience of locals sat at the tables, watching the scene. They nodded and smiled at the Americans as they positioned themselves on a window seat.

'Everyone is friendly here,' Rose said.

'They don't worry me,' George said.

'Have you tried the cider here?' Rose enquired.

'I prefer the beer,' replied George, waving in Barney's direction.

The landlord nodded and carried over a tray of drinks. 'You'll be all right now Mr Lestrange', he said, 'now you have found the ladies.'

'Surely am, Barney,' George laughed, expansively. 'Have a drink yourself, and everyone here.'

'Right neighbourly of you, sir,' Barney replied warmly, making his way back to the bar.

Various old men raised their hats politely or waved their gnarled walking-sticks in the direction of their benefactor, as they sat at their tables and waited for their pints to be delivered to them by Barney.

'Now, you tell us, George', Rose commanded, 'when did you arrive in Barfield?'

'Yesterday afternoon,' George replied. 'I've been getting to know everyone. What a cute little place!'

'They think we are all mad,' Rose explained. 'Why didn't you let us know you were arriving. We could have delayed our trip to London.'

'I came on an impulse,' said George. 'We can finish our vacation together. I want to spend the rest of my life with you.'

'George, you embarrass me,' protested Rose.

'All right, you two,' said Amie. 'Looks like I have been the cause of your being parted. I am feeling better now and want to thank you for your care.' Looking at Rose, she squeezed her hand.

'Are you really better?' George asked her. 'Your mother was worried when you had that little trouble.'

'Surely, I am truly recovered,' Amie smiled. 'Now why don't you two get married?'

George turned to Rose. 'I don't know your daughter very well yet, but she sure has some good ideas.'

'Come back to the house and we can have dinner together,' Rose told George. 'I am sure someone here can ask Elsie to return to cook for us.' Barney, in his Aran sweater and cords, leaned comfortably on the bar and nodded in reply.

Chapter Thirty-Seven

George accompanied Rose and Amie back to the house. When he saw the house, he exclaimed, 'What a quaint little shack! I could just wrap the whole lot up and put in my backyard.'

'You don't have a backyard, George,' Rose reminded him.

'You are too pedantic,' George protested. 'I can always use my little place way out in the sticks.'

Amie ran to the front door and put her key in the lock. The engaged couple followed her in, and soon they were seated in the lounge, drinking coffee.

'We can stay in quietly this evening and talk,' Rose suggested, cuddling up to her man.

Amie laughed. 'I can go to bed early. I have some writing to catch up on.'

Ernie's cab drew up noisily in the cul-de-sac. Elsie entered by way of the front door.

'What can I get you for dinner, dear,' she called out as she made her way past the open lounge door and into the kitchen. 'Ernie is going to cut the grass. I'll make the tea and take him some. Do you like steak and kidney pie, Mr Lester? I make a lovely one. Then, what about a nice rhubarb crumble?'

The group of Americans in the lounge looked at each other and chuckled.

'I can see who is the boss in this house,' George whispered hoarsely.

Outside in the garden, Ernie was rattling about with the mower. Inside in the kitchen, Elsie sat on the chair and eased her feet into her comfy slippers. Rose and George opened the french windows, stepped through, and made a tour of the garden's trees and plants. Amie went out through the garden door and headed for her favourite spot.

There, under the leafy mantle, dappled by spots of sunlight piercing the branches above her, Amie settled herself on the rustic swing. The leaves on the ground were disturbed by her heels making ruts in them as she swung to and fro. No grass grew in that leafy shade; only ancient moss clung to the gnarled tree roots. Although the young woman had only recently come to live in this abode, she instinctively knew this was her place to relax and think.

For instance, there was this news of her mother's engagement. Why had she not thought of the possibility before? This showed how selfish she was. Surely she had used her mother's good nature and unselfishness without considering her feelings. The house she had lived in since her divorce was owned by her mother. The housekeeper and babysitter was her mother. Amie felt a twinge of regret. Hardly ever had she considered the fact that her mother needed a life of her own and was not there to be used just because she was a widow and over fifty.

Then there was the business of Robert James. All this time she had taken him for granted, too. When he had been hovering there in the background, he had been a nuisance, spoiling her fun. Then, when he was no longer there, she had been hurt and spoke out sharply when he did make an appearance. All the while he had been working behind the scenes to make her happy.

Amie thought guiltily of the shipboard affair, on which she had embarked on the way to England. Even at the time she knew this was wrong and a product of her restless spirit caused by her nervous breakdown. Now she felt even worse now that she knew who had really arranged her trip. Should she tell Robert what had happened on the ship? There was no need. After all they were not going to get married. Who would want to marry her, a divorced woman who had had two affairs during the past year? Then again, there had been no one else in the four years since her divorce.

Then there was Poppy. What man would want to take on someone else's child? Amie paused. What was she prattling about? Just because Robert admired her and had kissed her once or twice, did not mean a proposal was in the offing. He had disappeared twice since meeting her in England.

What she must do, Amie decided, was to devote more time to her responsibility as Poppy's mother. When the vacation was finished, she must return to America and devote herself to making her living and providing a good home for her little girl.

Amie gradually realised that Rose was walking towards her with George. Their voices drifted through the swaying branches obscuring the swing.

'This is a wonderful spot for you to relax in,' said George. 'For Amie to come back to her senses, too.'

'No need to talk like that,' said Rose. 'The poor girl has been through a lot and is almost back to normal.'

'Sorry, sweetheart,' apologised George. 'I have missed you so much and anything that gets in the way annoys me.'

'Soon we'll be together,' promised Rose. 'In every way, darling.'

There was a silence as they embraced and kissed. Amie was petrified with embarrassment and held the swing as still as possible. They must not know she was eavesdropping. The long moment continued for what seemed eternity.

Their feet could be seen on the path beyond the branches. Eventually the feet turned to walk away. The distant murmur of voices gave a clue to their whereabouts. They must be sitting on the rustic seat in the little arbour.

Amie crept out from her refuge and crept furtively down the garden and into the house through the back door. Elsie was busily cooking.

Trying to creep in past her was useless. 'Creamy custard and new potatoes with mint, does that suit you, Miss?' Elsie demanded.

'Sounds delicious,' Amie agreed absent-mindedly.

Ernie had finished mowing the lawn, and had been roped in to shell the peas. He nodded, morosely, preferring to be pottering about in the garden.

'Would you like to chop the mint or mix the custard, Miss?' asked Elsie.

'Later on,' replied Amie. 'I must have a bath and change my clothes after that train journey.'

Elsie sniffed with pique and adjusted her pinny around her ample waist.

Amie ran upstairs and locked herself in the bathroom. Quickly she shed her clothes and threw them in a heap on the tiled floor. Bubbles piled themselves up in perfumed heaps in the bath. They enveloped her as she slid her naked body down into the fragrant froth.

Now she had time to think. George had certainly made his feelings clear. He thought she should pull herself together. Well, she did intend to, although these things took time. He must realise that. That had already been decided. There had been no pretence on her part. Many hurtful occurrences, both physical and mental, had happened to her. The past was gone. The future was all that mattered for her and Poppy. What about the two lovebirds, then? Rose and her boyfriend were certainly serious about each other. How wonderful to have someone to love you so much. Amie wished happiness for them both!

Rose tapped at the bathroom door. 'You have been in there ages,' she called out. 'Let me have a quick bath while you entertain George.'

Amie could not tell her she had been on the swing for most of the time. 'I'll entertain him,' she laughed. 'Just wait until I get some clothes on.'

Reluctantly stepping from the bubbles, she patted herself dry with the soft bath towel and ran into her room to dress in fresh underwear and a white blouse and long black skirt. Slipping some high-heeled slippers on, she walked downstairs, tying her hair back with a ribbon. George stood up as she walked into the lounge. He took her hands in his.

'We haven't spent much time together,' he said. 'I hope we can be friends, as I am going to marry your mother.'

Amie reached up to kiss him on the cheek. 'That's wonderful news, for all of us,' she said. 'I hope you are going to be really happy.'

Chapter Thirty-Eight

Elsie looked round the door and said, 'Dinner's ready when you are. Tell Miss Rose to hurry up.' Amie poured George a drink.

Rose soon appeared down the stairs, freshly bathed and wearing an ivory silk shirt and black satin trousers. 'That dinner smells delicious!' she enthused. 'My mouth is watering.'

'Someone can lay the table,' commanded Elsie. 'Ernie and me can have ours out here in the kitchen. You don't mind, Miss, do you? There was too much for just you.'

'No, of course not,' agreed Rose, smiling as she took the white tablecloth from the sideboard drawer. 'Pull the table out, George.'

Amie retrieved the cutlery from the black box. Soon everyone was tucking in to the delicious English cooking. When they had finished, George went out into the kitchen. 'That was marvellous, Elsie', he said, 'you have got to marry me!'

Elsie shrieked with laughter. 'You are a humorous gentleman, Mr Lester, you made our Ernie laugh, too,' she chuckled, indicating the heaving shoulders of her snorting nephew. 'Any more rhubarb crumble and custard?'

'I have already had two helpings,' George said, patting his stomach. 'Look at my waistline.'

'Fine figure of a man like you sir,' said Elsie soothingly. 'You just need feeding up a bit!'

Rose and Amie came out into the kitchen, carrying the used plates.

'Elsie, that was wonderful,' said Rose. 'Oh, I forgot, I brought a present back for you from London.'

Elsie smiled broadly as Rose brought a little packet in from the lounge and handed this to her. Inside was a little cameo brooch.

'Why, that is beautiful, Miss Rose,' said Elsie. 'Go lovely on my neckline, like.' Carefully, she pinned the brooch centrally below her collar. 'Mother thought the scarf was beautiful, too,' she continued. 'Says she'll keep that for special occasions.'

'Tell her to wear the scarf often,' Rose decreed. 'I want her to use my gift.'

'I'll do that, love,' Elsie agreed. 'Now let's get tidied up and I can leave you folks in peace.'

Everyone joined in clearing up. The dishes were stacked in the dishwasher. Ernie ambled into the garden to put away the tools. Elsie tidied the kitchen and they went home.

'I like to keep the place tidy for Mr Robert,' she said. *As if she were expecting him at any moment,* thought Amie.

'We have had a long day,' said Amie. 'I'm for bed.'

Darkness was upon the garden and the trees rustled secretly as the evening breeze made a last circuit of the garden. At the end of the path the front gate creaked and rattled forlornly.

Rose and George said goodnight to Amie, and settled themselves in front of the television. They did not watch much television as they found they could not kiss at the same time. Kissing won. Being apart for so long had been a torment for them.

Rose crossed the room to draw the curtains, making the room look cosier. George followed her to the window. 'Did I tell you how lovely you look tonight?' he asked. 'I couldn't wait to squeeze you tight like this.' He caught her in a bear-hug.

'I hope you don't plan to stay the night,' she said. 'With Amie upstairs, I feel awkward.'

'We can't go to my room at The King's Head, either,' said George. 'Everyone within ten miles would know by morning and your reputation would be ruined.'

'Positively true,' sighed Rose. 'You can stay here a while, though.'

'I had to travel a long way to find you again, you gorgeous thing,' George whispered in her ear, pulling her down on to the sofa. 'All that waiting made me impatient.'

'I am glad you did travel here,' Rose replied softly, holding him close. 'Only last night I was writing to you, asking you to come and see me.'

'Your wish has come true, honeybun,' said George, kissing her neck. 'I am here now.'

'Hush!' cautioned Rose. 'Don't make too much noise.'

Upstairs, Amie was lying in bed, watching the night sky through the branches which tapped at intervals on her bedroom window. How things had changed! Here was her mother entertaining a man friend downstairs. Meanwhile, her own daughter was thousands of miles away under another roof!

What of Robert James? He had done another of his disappearing acts. They had seemed to be getting on so well and were smoothing out their differences. Now he had vanished into thin air again.

Amie shifted restlessly in the bed and at last drifted off to sleep. Dreams came of being forced to climb a steep hillside. Someone was trying to bar her way as sticks and stones cut into her feet. Ahead of her a strong figure held out a hand, but could not reach her, saying, 'Remember, you can *do* what you *can* do.'

Someone moaning woke her up. Moonlight flooded in through the window and she was the one moaning. All that rich food, she muttered to herself, sitting up. Making me dream again.

Amie slipped out of bed and padded barefooted down the stairs to the kitchen. The house was in darkness but she did not feel nervous in the friendly atmosphere surrounding her. The ambience was a comfortable friend. This house reminded her of Robert; if only he were here. But why had she thought that?

Rose was in bed and George had gone back to The King's Head hours ago. They were lucky, being together and being in love, while she was alone. The light in the kitchen glared in her eyes. A few sips of water and she would return to bed.

This time she slept easily and awoke to daylight. Rose brought coffee up to her and a letter from Poppy and another from Betty Steiner, her friend from the swimming party where all this had begun. Poppy's letter was full of her doings and cute little drawings. Betty's was full of gossip also the information that John Peters and Joanne Webber had married last week.

Apparently the wedding had been the most expansive anyone could remember seeing and the happy couple had flown off to Bermuda for their honeymoon. Amie wondered whether her friend was trying to upset her with this news or was simply forewarning her to prevent any sudden shock.

Amie found she did not care either way. In fact, she had no feelings about those two. They were past history. Best to forget that foolish part of her life.

Remembering her resolutions of the night before, Amie dressed and hurried downstairs. 'Mom,' she called. 'You go see George and leave the work to me.'

Rose was indeed already on the point of leaving. 'I'm just going to see George,' she said. 'He is expecting me.'

The door closed briskly behind her. Amie was left to her own devices. There was only the swing to comfort her. Then a cat, waiting outside the back door, began to meow plaintively.

Amie went out into the garden, strolled down the path and eased herself onto the swing. The cat followed her and jumped up onto her lap, purring deeply. 'Hello, cat,' she said, stroking the velvet-smooth black coat of the wiry animal as she swung slowly to and fro. 'Where do you live?'

'You have met my cat, I see,' came a quiet voice.

Startled, she looked up. 'Must you always creep up on me?' she asked Robert James. There he stood, just outside the barrier of branches, looking through the gaps between the leaves. The cat made a shrill chirruping noise in her throat as if she had swallowed the blue bird of happiness.

Chapter Thirty-Nine

Robert stepped into the arbour and picked up the cat from Amie's lap. He rubbed the cat's soft face against his and put her down on the ground. 'Now stand on the swing,' he told Amie. Bemused, she did so, holding on to the ropes.

'This makes me the same height as you,' said Amie.

'How observant of you,' said Robert, 'Now I must hold you near, so that you do not fall off.'

He held her so tight she could not move. His face was so close to hers that they were breathing the same air. The swing creaked gently beneath her feet. Their lips blended in a long kiss and she wondered how she had managed to live without him before this moment.

'This is rather a surprise,' panted Amie, as she came up for air.

'You don't mind, do you?' asked Robert, shifting his position slightly. Amie shook her head, her heart thundering in her chest.

Robert sighed and wrapped his arms tighter around her. 'Where have you been?' Amie asked him.

'Sorry I had to rush off the other day,' said Robert, kissing her cheek. 'I had to go home to sort something out. Your face is so soft! I hope you don't mind all this. Tell me if you want me to stop. I could go on holding you forever. I have realised, my dear, that I have done all this without asking. You do like me, don't you?'

'Robert, I think I love you,' replied Amie. 'I feel as if I have lost and then found you again.'

'Good show,' muttered Robert, covering her mouth with his as he slid his hands beneath her top and caressed her back.

Amie felt the sharp movement of the swing as the cat jumped up next to her feet. The cat rubbed her soft sinewy body against the young woman's bare legs, increasing the sensations she was feeling from her top half. A deep vibrant purring rumbled from the cat's throat. Reluctantly, Robert relinquished his embrace and looked down at the swing.

Round amber eyes stared up at him unblinkingly, then winked, owlishly, at him. Robert reached down and picked up the cat. He helped her on to his shoulder, where she perched, like a feline parrot. Amie jumped down from the swing and they walked, side by side and in silence, back to the house.

Once they had entered through the back door, the cat jumped down on to the kitchen stool. 'Can you guess her name?' asked Robert. Amie shook her head. 'Captain Flint – you know, from *Treasure Island*.'

Amie nodded, with understanding. 'Because she sits on your shoulder,' she said. 'Where does she go when you're not here?'

'The neighbours take her in,' said Robert. 'When I come back from my travels, she seems to know, and reappears.'

'That means she is like her master, disappearing and reappearing. Anyway, surely she is the wrong sex for her name.'

'How do you know what sex a parrot is?' retorted Robert. 'I know what *you* are though, darling.' He slid his arms round her and kissed her forehead.

'When we kissed in the park in London', said Amie, 'I thought you were having fun but you have followed me here.'

Robert kissed her nose. 'That was great fun', he said, 'I am also very serious. Why can't you understand how I feel? Also I came here because I live here sometimes and wanted to see Captain Flint again.' He chuckled.

'My trouble is that I can't believe what anyone says any more,' said Amie. 'After everything that has happened, and some things you don't know about, I can never expect anyone to love me.' Miserably, she lowered her eyes.

'I told you before,' Robert told her abruptly. 'From the moment I saw you there was no one else for me. When you were involved with that swine, John Peters, all I could do was to be there to help. I endured your disposition stoically. I worried when you were missing and injured. Then I was forced to leave and did not know whether to visit you but decided I had better not. The news of your nervous breakdown did not reach me until later. All I could do was let you know I was thinking of you. Later on I had the chance of making my home available for your use.'

Amie moved away from him and put the kettle on for coffee. 'Shall we sit down to discuss this?' she asked.

Robert put a saucer of milk down for Captain Flint. He opened the cupboard and took out a tin of sardines, which he opened with the attached key and tapped into a dish for the cat. Then he crossed the room to Amie and put his arm round her. 'Make mine tea and biscuits,' he said. 'I could never really get used to coffee and doughnuts.'

Amie made the tea and the two of them went into the lounge and sat together on the sofa. They sipped their tea and nibbled their biscuits. Robert blew on his hot drink, impatiently. His hand rested lightly on her knee.

'Did you know my mother's friend came over from America to visit her?' asked Amie.

'Yes, Elsie told me,' replied Robert.

'So you saw Elsie before you saw me!' said Amie in mock surprise.

'No, she spotted me driving through Barfield and interrogated me,' said Robert. 'That family has been on the estate for generations and know us better than we know ourselves.'

'This is very grand,' said Amie, anxious now as she put her tea cup on the table. 'Sometimes I forget and then you remind me again of your position.'

'I'm still myself and I know what position I want to be in,' Robert replied his voice becoming harsh with emotion. 'I fed Captain Flint to keep her quiet, so now come with me!'

He took her by the hand and led her to the stairs. 'Where are we going?' Amie asked.

'Which one is your room?' Robert answered her by means of another question, leading her up the stairs.

'The little back one,' Amie replied.

'I thought you would have that one,' Robert commented. 'I imagined you asleep in there at night when I was restless.'

'Did you?' Amie was surprised. 'I thought of you too, and even had bad dreams.'

'You must not have bad dreams', Robert said, 'only good ones, of me.'

Amie stood on tiptoes on the landing to kiss his mouth. 'If you love me, I shall,' she promised.

Robert led her into her room and sat on her bed. He lay down and held her pillow to his face. 'I can smell your perfume,' he breathed softly. 'You must sleep sweetly after this!'

Amie snuggled down happily next to him and rested her arm happily on his chest. 'I shall always have you to remember,' she said.

Robert turned to her and drew her towards him. 'This is lovely, to lie like this with you,' he whispered in her ear, pulling her body towards him. 'I know your mother has gone to visit Mr Lestrange, and I have bribed Captain Flint to keep out of the way, so we have the house to ourselves!'

'Wonderful, I can't think of anything I would rather do,' said Amie.

'I can!' said Robert, swinging his long legs to the carpeted floor and sitting on the edge of the bed. 'Stand up for a minute, darling.' He reached down to undo his laces and took off his shoes and socks.

'To think that last night I woke up, longing for you!' exclaimed Amie, standing in front of him, 'and here you are, in the flesh.'

Robert gently removed Amie's clothes, until she stood shyly before him. He sighed deeply, then rested his face against her neck and ran his hands down the contours of her body.

Chapter Forty

'May I make love to you, darling?' asked Robert, humbly. He drew her down to the bed.

'Of course you may,' replied Amie. With fumbling fingers, she undid his shirt buttons. His chest was more muscular than his height suggested and she lay against him, skin to skin. This caused Robert to perspire and to remove his clothes as rapidly as possible.

After Robert had held Amie close in his arms, kissed and caressed and made love to her tenderly, yet passionately, he whispered in her ear, 'Darling, do say you'll marry me.'

Amie looked into his eyes, the glow of love still on her face, and replied, 'Robert, I don't know. There is so much to think about.'

Robert sighed, pulling the sheet up over them. They went to sleep, locked in each other's arms. The day drifted on through afternoon until Captain Flint, bored with licking out the last vestiges in the sardine tin and clean in paws and whiskers, came upstairs to find them.

Captain Flint looked in the bedroom door and saw the two human forms lying beneath the sheet. Of course there was no understanding the mad behaviour of humans, but at least they should know the right time to go to bed! That was at night, while cats were out, hunting in the dark. They must be awakened...

Captain Flint leaped lightly onto the bed and tedded sharply through the sheet, clawing into Robert's leg and meowing loudly.

Robert jumped up suddenly, clutching at his leg. 'Captain Flint, you witch!' he exclaimed.

Amie, woken by the sudden commotion, sat up in bed, surprised for the moment to find others in her room. Realisation of what had happened came to her and she turned to the man, seated at the end of her bed, examining the points of blood on his leg.

'Hello, there,' she said.

Robert looked at her and smiled. 'Hello, there, yourself,' he said. 'Come on, let's go for a shower to wake us up. Captain Flint has already started the process.'

He took her by the hand and led her downstairs. Pausing only to let Captain Flint out of the back door, he went into the shower room next to the coats cupboard and switched on the shower. Amie felt herself being pulled into the water and shuddered at the coldness. Robert shut the door behind them and wrapped his companion in his arms in the cleansing stream of water.

Amie stood there, torn between the enjoyment of being one with her lover and the wish to escape from the torment of cold water. After a few minutes the ordeal was over. Robert switched off the shower and wrapped the young woman in a large fluffy towel, with which he commenced to pat her dry.

Soon they were both towelled off and feeling invigorated by the experience. 'Nothing like a cold shower,' said Robert, briskly.

'You beast,' complained Amie, punching his chest ineffectually. He fended off her blows easily.

'Look in here, darling,' said Robert, opening the door of the coats cupboard. 'Did you know these were my mackintosh and boots in here?'

'Well, I do now,' replied Amie.

Robert led the way upstairs. 'By the way, my love', he said, 'what time does your mother get back?'

Amie wrinkled her forehead in thought. 'I have no idea,' she replied.

'Well, here we are, starkers,' said Robert.

They ran upstairs and went into Amie's golden room. Robert picked her up and dropped her onto the bed. He bent down to kiss her waiting mouth. They giggled happily as they wrestled playfully; the conclusion being more love making. This time their desire led to fulfilment in a more leisurely manner. There was no need for the frantic rapture of their previous intimacy.

Whilst lying in Robert's arms afterwards, Amie looked at her bedside clock. 'Six o'clock!' she exclaimed. 'I must get dressed.'

Robert lay there, watching her dress herself. 'You are so wonderful,' he said. 'I could watch you forever.'

He sat up and pulled her towards him, holding her in his arms and kissing her. So, with interruptions, they managed to put their clothes on.

The sound of the key rattling in the front door made them jump. 'You should wait downstairs,' said Amie, in a panic. The phone began ringing in the lounge.

'We have no reason to feel guilty,' said Robert, walking deliberately down the stairs.

Rose came in through the front door as Robert picked up the phone. 'George wants to speak to you,' he told her.

'Why, I didn't expect to see you here,' she said. 'I have just left him, as well.'

Robert walked into the kitchen and put the kettle on. Amie came down the stairs, having combed her hair and applied lipstick to her tender lips; tender through too much kissing. He grabbed her hand as she entered the room and pulled her towards him. They almost began kissing again but moved apart.

'I missed you immediately,' said Amie softly.

'So did I, my darling,' said Robert gently.

Rose called out from the lounge, 'So, what brings you here, Robert?'

'He came to see whether we had arrived back safely,' said Amie. Together, she and Robert carried the coffee into the lounge. 'What made George ring you so soon?' she continued, craftily changing the subject.

'He wants to take us out for dinner tonight. Why don't you come with us, Robert?' replied Rose. 'By the way, Amie, your hair looks damp.'

'I would be charmed to have dinner with you,' said Robert.

'I had a shower earlier,' said Amie almost simultaneously, exchanging glances with Robert.

'Why are you two acting so weirdly?' asked Rose. 'Have you any secrets?'

'May I tell her?' Robert asked Amie. He put his arm round her shoulders and squeezed her, reassuringly.

'There is nothing to tell,' Amie hissed at him, embarrassed.

Rose darted a sharp glance at them and left the room. Obviously, something was going on there. This had been the wrong moment to return. If she had known Robert was here she would have returned later but she had thought Amie was alone in the house.

Robert appeared perplexed as Amie moved away from him. Crossing the room to the french windows, she stood, looking out at the garden. He followed her across the room to stand behind her. His hand automatically moved to rest comfortingly on her shoulder.

'I am so sorry,' said Robert. 'I seem to have said the wrong thing. My mind and body were overwhelmed by you. You cannot feel the same, apparently.'

'Oh, but I do,' said Amie, turning to face him and holding his long slim hands in her own small ones. 'I just can't face going into another relationship. Everything I do turns to failure. If we tried and failed, I would be devastated.'

'There is no guarantee of anything in this world,' said Robert. 'We must take happiness while we can. You are my happiness. Look, come with me to visit my mother. That is where I went last night. To tell her about us, I mean.'

'You didn't!' said Amie, horrified. 'I haven't promised you anything yet.'

'Good Lord!' exclaimed Robert. 'So you haven't said "yes"? I was so clear in my own mind that we agreed, and I cannot believe we can be parted now.'

'You might think I was on the rebound,' said Amie. 'I've just heard of the wedding of John and Joanne, from Betty in America.

Chapter Forty-One

Robert replied by taking her elbows in his hands and lifting her up to his level so that he could kiss her on the lips. 'You would not respond to me so passionately if you were on the rebound,' he said. 'If I thought you were still keen on John Peters, there is no way I would want you. I knew of their wedding but did not think you knew yet. All that is irrelevant.'

Amie swallowed hard and took a deep breath. 'Would you ask me again?' she queried. 'Please, darling.'

Robert found he was trembling with emotion as he knelt before her. 'Dearest, would you make me the happiest man in the world and become my wife?' he asked.

Amie touched his face gently with her hand. 'I would love to,' she said, her voice quavering. 'I want to be your wife.'

Robert stood up, kissed her hand and then her lips. 'Thank you,' he said, huskily. 'I shall always be faithful to you.'

Amie was laughing and crying at the same time as they hugged each other. Robert felt exhilaration beyond anything he had ever felt before.

'Don't you think this is all a bit sudden?' Amie asked him, her head resting against his chest. 'I don't know what everyone is going to say.'

'A lot can happen in a day,' said Robert, stroking her hair. 'Anyway, I expect the whole of Barfield has been busily laying bets on when we were going to name the day.'

Amie sighed. 'There was something about you from the beginning,' she said. 'You were always there in the background. That was what irritated me, having you there, but out of reach. I needed you to be close, more substantial.'

Robert kissed her tenderly and went to the drinks cabinet. 'I am substantial enough,' he answered her. 'Now for the toast. We have no champagne,' he added. 'Wine must do for the time being.'

A voice came from upstairs. 'Can I come down yet, you two?'

'Come down Mom, we are drinking a toast,' called Amie.

Rose entered the room, an expectant look on her face.

'This time we *do* have something to tell you,' said Robert. 'Amie has agreed to marry me.'

'Oh my, what a surprise,' said Rose. 'You sure kept this relationship quiet back in America.'

'We didn't know then we were going to marry,' explained Amie.

'I am taking Amie to meet my mother,' said Robert. 'The morning will be soon enough. We would be pleased to meet you and George for dinner tonight. Then we can celebrate the engagement.'

Robert left the house to get ready for the dinner party. He too was staying at The King's Head. The atmosphere he left behind him was anticlimactic. Rose did not know what to think; the moody, unhappy daughter she had left in the house that morning had been transformed into a radiant, happy creature, and engaged to a lord, of all things.

Of course she had seen their flushed faces and noticed their secret smiles to each other when she came in the house. After all, they were not the only ones to be in love.

But the suddenness of their declaration had been a surprise. Rose thought Amie must have loved the man without admitting the fact to herself.

That evening, Robert arrived with George at the house. There were hugs and kisses all round and the quartet went out to a country hotel, the White Hart, to celebrate the engagement. They were driven by a chauffeur in Robert's Rolls-Royce. Amie was relaxed and radiant at last. Rose was relieved to see her daughter happy and off her hands.

They dined in a beautiful period dining room. The furniture was of dark stained wood. On the tables lay cloths of white linen, and beautiful crimson and gold flower arrangements graced the centre of each one. Above their heads, the ceiling was low and white, patterned by heavy blackish beams.

Long midnight blue curtains framed the mullioned windows. The diners' feet sank into the deep-piled ultramarine carpet. Little lanterns hung from the walls all round the room, shedding a white light. On each table, in the centre of the flower arrangement, a tall scarlet candle took pride of place.

The waiter greeted Robert effusively and showed the party to their table. He took the ladies' coats as he helped them with their chairs. George looked round appreciatively. Rose and Amie were in their most elegant dresses: fitted royal blue satin with a matching bolero for the mother, and shell pink full-skirted taffeta with bare shoulders and narrow straps decorated with marcasites for the daughter.

Robert took the wine list from the waiter and had an earnest discussion with him. 'Just ordering something special for the occasion – but first we shall have champagne,' he said, smiling at Amie. 'This must be a double engagement party,' generously including Rose and George in his celebrations.

Rose laughed and took George's hand. 'That's all right, Robert,' she said. 'We already had a double engagement party with Wanda and Fred, way back in LA,' and glanced at Amie.

'I did not know this,' protested Amie.

'Baby, you were much too weak to be told anything,' explained Rose. 'You were in hospital and not to be upset.'

Amie became solemn for a moment, then smiled at Robert. 'If you had been there,' she began.

Robert took her hand. 'I wish I had been,' he assured her.

'All's well that ends well,' said George, realising he had not yet contributed anything to the conversation. 'I must say you ladies look really lovely.' They both nodded their thanks.

The waiter returned with the champagne in an ice bucket. He extracted the cork, with the customary popping explosion, poured some into a glass and stood with his head slightly to one side while Robert tasted the sparkling wine and indicated his assent. A waitress approached, bringing giant menus and handed one to each of the diners. Then she stood back slightly, waiting for their orders.

The waiter poured the champagne into the other glasses and discreetly lit the candle. When the choices of food had been made the toasts began, wishing each other long and happy marriages. The first bottle was rapidly consumed. When the main course arrived, Robert beckoned to the waiter, who brought the wine he had selected earlier.

'This is a wonderful dinner you are giving us,' said Rose. 'I can't remember when I had such a lovely evening out.'

'Yes, you're a wonderful guy,' said George. 'You must let me pay.'

'Nonsense, that's all right,' said Robert. 'This is to thank you for looking after my Amie and bringing her safely to me.'

'Oh, that is a sweet thing to say,' murmured Rose, dabbing at her eyes with her white linen serviette.

Amie had been thoughtful for some time and now broke her silence. 'I want to thank you all for looking after me,' she said. 'Mom, you have nursed me through my illness and put up with my moods and George, you have been a good friend.'

Robert looked at her ruefully, 'What about me, darling,' he hinted.

'I'll tell you that later,' said Amie, blushing.

The evening continued happily but none of them wished to stay out too late. Amie and Robert were travelling early in the morning. They walked out into the chill night air. Outside the hotel, the Rolls-Royce awaited them.

'I never thought I'd ride in one of these!' Rose said, thrilled.

'This is a really dignified way to travel,' George agreed.

Robert helped Amie into the back seat and got in himself. The chauffeur drove away and the passengers settled back to enjoy the luxurious ride.

'I don't ride about in this all the time,' whispered Robert in Amie's ear, taking the opportunity to nibble at her earlobe. 'This is only to impress you.'

Chapter Forty-Two

When Amie was back at her holiday home and safe in her bed, she reminisced on the events of the previous two days. That so much had happened did not seem at all possible. The past was a dim memory, overwhelmed by the promise of the future. What stupendous luck for her that such an understanding yet strong-minded man as Robert James loved her and had waited for her.

Earlier that day he had shared this very bed with her. Tingles ran up and down her spine at the thought. Now she knew what a tender and passionate lover he was. Soon they would be married and she would stay in England with him.

Next day Amie woke early to the songs of her bird friends outside. Robert had told her to wear something simple. A look through her wardrobe produced a limited choice. The eventual selection she made was a cotton shift dress and jacket in pale turquoise, his favourite colour.

'I'm going, Mom,' Amie called, running down the stairs.

'You look lovely, dear,' said Rose, who was already in the kitchen, making coffee. 'I can't believe you have done so well.'

'He is the man I want,' said Amie, 'nothing else.'

'Of course,' agreed Rose. 'Now have a great time, and don't let his mother condescend to you.'

Amie sat at the kitchen table and sipped her coffee. 'I was just thinking,' she confessed. 'There was this man on the ship. I must have been off my head. We had a mad fling.'

Rose patted her shoulder sympathetically. 'I knew about your involvement with him,' she said. 'Put that down to experience. I think that was part of your illness. Above all, not a word to Robert; no need for him to know.'

Amie looked up, sharply. 'So you knew all the time,' she said.

Rose sat down at the table opposite her. 'Yes, I thought he would be a good friend for you,' she said. 'That is, until I discovered he was married.'

'I was silly, but nothing seemed to matter then,' Amie mused.

'We all do silly things but the wise ones learn from their mistakes,' Rose philosophised.

'Didn't you think Robert looked smart in his dinner suit last night?' Amie asked.

'He is an elegant man,' Rose replied. 'Clothes become him well.'

There was a sharp rap at the front door. Rose looked through the window. The chauffeur was outside. Amie opened the door and handed some flowers in, then she was gone.

The mixed blooms were wrapped in pale mauve tissue-paper and the stems tied with deep purple satin ribbons. A card inside bore the message, *To my future mother-in-law*. What a thoughtful man! He would make a good husband for Amie in so many ways.

Rose arranged the flowers artistically in a vase on an oval highly-polished occasional table in the lounge, with the wrappings and card displayed adjacent to the pottery container. George would be arriving soon. They were spending the day together. With any luck they would not be disturbed.

Meanwhile, Robert and Amie were being driven to his mansion. As they passed through the hamlet of Barfield, the sturdy figure of Elsie could be seen, waving from the roadside. The car slid noiselessly to a standstill. The chauffeur swung his uniformed legs from the driver's seat and opened the passenger door.

'Good morning to you, Elsie,' said Robert, leaning out.

'Oh, Mr Robert, sir,' replied Elsie, hurrying towards him.

'Is there something wrong?' asked Robert with concern.

'Just so long as you are passing through, like,' explained Elsie. 'Would you be so kind as to look in on Mother, she being poorly and took to her bed, to cheer her up you know.'

'How did she know you were driving through this morning?' Amie asked him.

'Don't ask,' Robert replied. 'Country telegraph. I had better go to see her. You don't mind, do you darling?'

'Of course not, let's go,' Amie responded.

'I knew you'd make a good wife,' Robert commented, kissing her hand as he extricated his long legs from the car.

Amie followed him and they trod the rough path to the cottage. Elsie lifted the latch to open the door and led the way into the dim interior. The curtains were closed. There was no sound but the slow tick-tock of the large clock on the mantelpiece.

The two shiny brown porcelain dogs glowered ob-scurely down. On the white tablecloth, covering the rustic table, sat the bright blue pottery vase, scattering petals from the drooping wild flowers, which were well past their best.

'Excuse the untidy room', said Elsie, 'I haven't had time.'

Elsie led the way into a little back bedroom, where her mother was resting in her bed by the window. The old lady was sitting up, her beloved fat tabby cat in her arms. There was a shawl round her shoulders, covering her voluminous flannelette nightdress. A home-made nutmeg brown rag rug lay by the bed on the linoleum-covered floor.

'Has the doctor been to see your mother?' asked Robert.

'Oh yes, Mr Robert, sir,' said Elsie. 'Says she has to rest; her age, you know. Nothing he can do.'

'Look, Flora,' said Robert, loudly, into the ear of the old lady. 'I am going out now but shall come back to see you tomorrow.'

'Thank you, Master Robert,' replied Flora in a thin, needy voice. 'Used to know your grandfather years ago.'

As the old lady looked out of the window at the pink blossoms on the apple trees, her red-rimmed eyes filled with tears. Robert bent his tall frame to kiss the old woman's wrinkled face. Elsie walked quickly from the room, dabbing at her eyes with her apron. The fat cat gazed contentedly around him and purred loudly.

'I'll soon see you up and about,' said Robert, holding the old lady's hand.

'I still got the scarf the foreign lady gave me,' said Flora, reaching out and taking the red and gold silk square from the little chest of drawers by the bed. 'This is for best.'

'Mom brought her that from London,' said Amie, softly. Leaning forward, she removed the shawl from the old lady's shoulders and placed the silk square there instead. 'There, that is cooler for you,' she said. Robert led her from the room.

'Don't worry, I'll be back soon,' said Robert, as they said farewell to Elsie, who congratulated them on their engagement.

'How does she know?' said Amie.

Soon the engaged couple were speeding along the main road. The dreaded meeting with his mother loomed in the near future.

'I feel responsible for them, you know,' said Robert seriously. 'Their family has served us for many years and deserves our respect.'

'I hadn't realised what tradition there is in England,' said Amie. 'We Americans have such a young country.'

'I was rather hoping this was to be your country, too,' said Robert.

'Sorry, I don't find this easy to take in,' said Amie. 'Say, how far away is your place?'

'Only about twenty miles,' said Robert. 'Don't worry, Mother is going to love you.'

Amie began to feel nervous. This house was a long way off. In her mind she had thought of a big house down the road a way. Hopefully this was not going to be some sort of a marble palace.

Chapter Forty-Three

As the Rolls-Royce purred noiselessly along, Amie began to relax. Robert glanced at her and took her hand. Squeezing his hand in return, she looked through the car window at the green fields sliding by. How much did she really know about him?

One minute they were – that is she was – at daggers drawn and now they were like two lovebirds. All too soon the journey was completed and they were slowing down in order to turn smoothly on to a road, flanked by titanic trees ensconced on high grassy banks; all this providing a frame for enormous open wrought-iron gates. As the car purred through, Amie turned her head to look back at the two tall gateposts, surmounted by fearsome stone lions.

'Is this the driveway?' asked Amie, nervously.

'We are nearly there, darling,' replied Robert.

They were soon moving between tall, sculpted hedges, which abruptly gave way to smooth lawns. In the distance, on a hill, was a massive grey mansion of weathered stone and brick. Between them and the building was a lake, surrounded by trees. Beyond this, the grass slope was bisected by the narrow white-ribbon of a path, which split at the top to circle a decorative fountain, only to join up again to meet the stone steps leading to the building.

'This cannot be real!' gasped Amie.

'An Englishman's home is his castle,' said Robert cheerfully. 'Welcome to mine, Fennstone.'

'This is so beautiful,' Amie declared.

'We are still quite a way off,' Robert told her. 'Might as well enjoy the view.'

There were woods to the right, inhabited by deer, as Robert said. Cultivated gardens could be seen to the left, with peacocks strutting between formal clipped hedges. In the distance a group could be seen moving along. Amie realised they were horses and riders.

'Everything is so immense,' said Amie, not yet recovered from the shock. 'Why didn't you tell me?'

'I wanted to see your reaction,' said Robert, tapping on the driver's partition. 'We shall walk from here.'

The car had navigated the path round the lake and now slowed to a halt. On the hill above them loomed the mansion. The chauffeur got out to open the door for them. Robert extricated himself first, then helped Amie to alight.

Robert took Amie by the hand and they began the walk up the path to the building.

'Are those your horses?' Amie asked.

'They belong to the Estate,' Robert replied. 'We hire them out and stable some, you know, everything helps.'

They reached the massive, intricately carved front door, which was flanked by white columns. A silver-haired man, wearing a dark morning suit, opened the door before anyone could ring. 'Good morning, my lord,' he said. 'I saw you approaching and took the liberty of coming out to meet you.'

'Good morning, Milton,' said Robert, stepping inside into the hall. 'This is my fiancée, Mrs Blake.'

'Happy to make your acquaintance, Mrs Blake,' said Milton, inclining his head slightly.

Amie stepped into the hallway, not knowing whether to shake hands or not. 'Happy to meet you, too,' she said.

Robert tossed his hat onto a branch of the antlers which decorated the ancient hat stand. 'Milton is our butler and general fount of all knowledge.'

'You are too kind, sir,' Milton protested.

'Would you look at that staircase!' Amie exclaimed, gazing upwards at the sweeping grandeur of the flight of stairs that led upward to the first floor.

'Is Mother ready to meet us?' Robert asked the butler.

'Madam is descending the stairs at this moment,' Milton replied.

The diminutive figure of a woman had appeared at the top of the stairs. Daintily, she began to walk slowly downstairs, flicking at the pleated skirt of her black silk suit with her fingers as she did so. The group at the bottom of the staircase became her captive audience. Robert walked towards her.

'Hallo, darling,' said the woman in a voice surprisingly strong for her size.

'Hello, Mother,' said Robert, bending to kiss her on the cheek.

'This must be Amie,' said the woman, proffering her hand.

Amie shook hands with her, trying to avoid all the rings on the older woman's fingers. 'Pleased to meet you,' she said.

'Do call me Grace,' said Robert's mother, leading the way into the drawing room and seating herself on a fragilely beautiful chaise longue.

'Milton has already made some coffee for you, as I expect that is what you prefer, being American.' The word American was pronounced 'foreigner'.

'I can drink either tea or coffee,' said Amie, offended.

'Rustle up some whisky, Milton,' said Robert. 'I feel the need.'

'Certainly, my lord,' said Milton. He left the room and soon returned with a glass and decanter on a tray.

'You are not drinking so early, dear!' protested Grace. 'Whatever is Amie going to think?'

'Nonsense, Mother,' said Robert. 'This is a special occasion.'

'Do sit down, Amie,' said Grace, patting the space next to her on the elegant brocade of the chaise longue.

Amie seated herself next to her hostess and accepted a cup of coffee from her. 'What a lovely coffee set,' she said. The tiny cups were of a dark green colour, rimmed with gold.

Grace fiddled with the silver milk and sugar set, rearranging them on the engraved silver tray, lying on the table in front of her. 'Yes, they are rather sweet,' she agreed casually.

Amie looked around the room at the burgundy curtains and deep red carpet. Meanwhile, Robert had poured himself a stiff whisky, and was standing rather self-consciously in front of the fireplace.

'Of course, we only live in one wing at the moment,' said Grace.

'Oh, really,' said Amie.

'I hope you two are going to get on,' interposed Robert nervously.

'Of course we are, dear,' replied Grace. 'So you are American, Amie?'

'From LA,' said Amie. 'My mother is over here with me.'

'How nice, you must bring her to meet me,' said Grace, patting her coiffured hair. 'So, Robert, your fiancée is a divorcee.' She said this as if 'divorcee' were a slightly naughty word.

'Well, what is wrong with that?' demanded Robert.

'Nothing, dear,' soothed Grace. 'What a shame your children went, too.' A lace handkerchief dabbed at her eyes served to indicate her sorrow.

'No need for that,' Robert said sharply. 'You don't want to upset everyone.' He cleared his throat.

'I'm sorry,' Amie said, looking down at the cup in her hand. 'Perhaps I shouldn't have come.'

'Forgive me,' Grace said, patting Amie's arm. 'I was thoughtless, but that accident still seems so recent. Lunch is in an hour. Why don't you two go for a walk whilst I lie down.'

'Good idea,' said Robert, 'come on.' He took Amie by the hand and hurried her out of the front door. They took the route on the left side, leading to the gardens. Behind one of the bushes he pulled her roughly to him, squeezing the breath out of her. 'I couldn't wait to hold you again,' he said. 'We have an hour.'

Chapter Forty-Four

'Do you think your mother dislikes me?' asked Amie, happy to be so close to Robert. 'All those not-so-subtle comments were hurtful.'

'You must not mind Mother,' said Robert, between kisses. 'I think Veronica's loss affected her more than anyone.'

'So why was that?' persisted Amie. 'They were your wife and children!'

'Veronica was a sort of second cousin and a favourite of Mother's,' said Robert. 'We were expected to marry and we knew this from childhood. You have to understand how things are here. I was never really in love with her but the accident was a terrible shock. When the children were lost too, everyone was devastated. You see, she was on her way to meet her boyfriend, as our marriage had been a sham for years.'

As Amie looked up at him with dismay and sympathy, there was a sudden screech behind her. Clutching at Robert's arms, she slowly turned her head to look round for the source of the noise. A marvellous sight met her eyes. There strutting proudly and displaying his wonderful metallic blue tail feathers was a magnificent peacock.

'Golly, he made me jump,' Amie complained. 'My, what a beautiful bird!'

'My old friend Solomon,' Robert declared. 'He of the thousand wives.'

Two of the peahens came haughtily into view, more dowdy than the male but still dignified. They uttered their strange meowing, echoing banshee sound as they approached, their legs moving with precision and heads held to one side, in order to discover what was going on.

Solomon released his tail feathers to form a train sweeping the grass behind him. He made his disdainful exit, with the two females following on. Robert led Amie down the path and on to a wide lawn. There were several other peacocks posing or walking to display their shimmering green plumage trains.

'They are so lovely,' Amie said. 'Poppy would love this.'

'Have you told her yet?' Robert asked. 'This is where she is going to live, unless you want her to go away to school.'

They sat on a bench to admire the peacocks. Amie tucked her hand into Robert's elbow and leaned her head on his shoulder. Truly she had not even considered her daughter's future. Everything had happened so quickly and no one had been told yet.

'We shall have to discuss that,' Amie decided. 'You don't mind taking on someone else's child, do you?'

'Of course not, darling,' Robert reassured her. 'By the way, we have not yet set a date.'

Amie reached up and kissed his cheek. 'As soon as possible,' she said, and asked, 'Do all the peacocks have names?' as another proud male paraded slowly past, showing his fine feathers.

Robert put his arm round her. 'All the boys are Solomon', he said, 'and all the girls are Sheba.' He closed her mouth with more kisses.

'There is a man watching us,' said Amie, presently, indicating a gnarled character, wearing a weather-beaten cap, leaning on his spade and scratching his head, in the middle-distance flower garden.

'That is only Jim, the gardener,' said Robert. 'We had better go in and freshen up for lunch.'

As they strolled away, a peahen followed behind them. Amie laughed and said, 'Goodbye, Sheba.'

The meal with Grace was a formal affair but Robert kept the tone light. He would not let his mother impose her authority on Amie. After they had eaten, they toured the big house. Only one wing was occupied by the family and the public had paid access to the rest of the mansion, on specified agreed days.

Grace kissed Amie goodbye on the cheek when they left. Robert thought she had softened towards the younger woman. Jennings, the chauffeur, drove the car smoothly away from the mansion. Through the back car window a little figure could be seen, dwarfed by the great carved doorway, waving her lace handkerchief and dwindling rapidly into the distance.

'You must not forget,' said Robert, holding Amie close in the privacy of the rear of the Rolls-Royce, 'when we are married, you are to be mistress of Fennstone. Mother can move to a cottage on the Estate or go to live with my sister. There are plenty of relatives. If she does stay, you are the boss, after me.'

The drive back to the holiday house went in a dream. Rose was not at home but Robert did not wait. He had to get back to Fennstone to make arrangements for the wedding. This was to take place as soon as possible, as neither of them wanted any delay.

Amie spent some time calling home. Everyone had to be informed, but mainly her daughter. Excited squeaks came down the line from the little girl. Amie's ex-husband Derek spoke to her and expressed amazement at the news, as if he were surprised she could get a man at all.

Poppy could not wait to come to England to be a bridesmaid, and travel would have to be arranged for her.

Friends needed to be informed. Amie contacted Wanda Merrington, who was thrilled at the tidings and would tell Fred Martin, who was now actually married to her. They had tied the knot earlier in the summer and were living at her place, until they could buy a larger house in the country.

Another friend Amie informed was Terrie Diamond at the office. The conversation was punctuated with giggles and the information that she and her boyfriend were getting hitched 'at any minute now'. Another important call was made to Betty Steiner. Amie invited her to come over for the wedding, for without her, none of this might have happened.

The only details she divulged were that he was a tall, quiet Englishman who had been working out there in America for a while, and was quite rich. They would know more later on. There was some satisfaction, however, in the fact that she now knew the news would get back to John Peters – who, she presumed, knew of Robert James's lineage.

When Rose arrived back with George, she was eager to hear of the events of the day. The fact of her friend Wanda's wedding was already known to her. They had been keeping in touch. The main thing now was to decide on the date.

Rose and George wanted to arrange their own ceremony to become man and wife. This was to happen soon. Things were becoming interesting. Everyone seemed to be jumping on the bandwagon and getting married at once.

Amie went down the garden to the swing for some peace and quiet. The cat – what was her name? Captain Flint, of course – appeared as if by magic and jumped up on her lap. The evening shadows made the little bower under the leaves into a dusky sanctuary.

'Where do you go when he is not here?' Amie asked the cat, tickling her neck and remembering the time not long ago, when Robert had appeared through the curtain of leaves and claimed her as his own.

Captain Flint made no reply. Amie slid down from the swing and carried the cat into the house. A saucer of milk on the kitchen floor sealed their bond. Elsie could always look after the cat while she and Robert were away on their honeymoon.

Thinking about Elsie reminded Amie of the old lady. Quickly crossing the hall to the lounge, she called The King's Head and asked the landlord how Flora was.

'Strange you should ask that,' mused Barney. 'Poor old girl passed away this afternoon. Long life she had. Must have been nigh a hundred.'

'Robert is going to be upset to hear that,' said Amie, tears springing to her eyes. 'I must speak to Elsie.'

'Elsie's gone to her relatives and Mr Robert already knows,' Barney divulged. 'We tell him everything first, Mrs Blake.'

'Well, thank you for the information,' Amie said, putting down the receiver. 'That put me in my place,' she told herself.

*

Later on, during their honeymoon and a year from their first meeting, Amie snuggled in Robert's arms. He held her close and told her he would never let her go. Responding to concerns she had expressed, he told her that the locals would soon grow to admire and respect her. In connection with her thoughts on a sibling for Poppy, he suggested trying right now.

Robert held Amie to him lovingly, saying, 'We are going to have a long and wonderful life together, with our children, at Fennstone.

'As someone of renown, namely Winston Churchill – who, as you know, had an American mother – once said, "Now this is not the end, this is not even the beginning of the end, but this is, perhaps, the end of the beginning!"'